the blinding light
A Sadie Gray Origin Story

R.B. Schow
Bailey James

RIVER CITY PUBLISHING

copyright

This book is licensed for your enjoyment only. This book may not be resold or given away to other people. If you are reading this book and did not purchase it, or it was not purchased for your use only, then please purchase a copy for yourself. Thank you for respecting the hard work of the author.

THE BLINDING LIGHT

Copyright © 2024 **R.B. Schow, Bailey James**. All rights reserved, including the right to reproduce this book, or portions thereof, in any form. No part of this text may be reproduced, transmitted, downloaded, decompiled, reverse-engineered, cloned, stored in, or introduced into any information storage or retrieval system in any form, or by any means, whether electronic or mechanical without the express written permission of the author. The scanning, uploading, and distribution of this book via the Internet or any other means without the express written permission of the author or publisher is illegal and punishable by law. Please purchase only authorized original or electronic editions and do not participate in or encourage electronic piracy of copyrighted materials.

Author's Note: This is a work of fiction. Names, characters, places, and incidents—and their usage for storytelling purposes—are crafted for the singular purpose of fictional entertainment and no absolute truths shall be derived from the information contained therein. Locales, businesses, events, government institutions, and private institutions are used for atmospheric, entertainment, and fictional purposes only. Furthermore, any resemblance or reference to an actual living person is used solely for atmospheric, entertainment, and fictional purposes.

The publisher does not have any control over, nor does it assume any responsibility for the author or third-party websites or their content.

For more information on the authors, their existing books, and upcoming releases, head to their website and take a look around: *www.SadieGrayBooks.com*.

one
sadie gray

LIFE WAS NEVER easy for my little sister or me, especially growing up. And then, one afternoon, right after we got off the bus to walk home one school day, it all got so much worse. When you're a fourteen-year-old girl, you have a beehive of thoughts swirling in your head: school, cute boys, all your friends, the mean girls and bullies, and your own physical, emotional, and mental awkwardness.

That's just for starters...

You also have family, chores, homework, and things like puberty and your period. These are all things you expect when growing up.

But what you don't always think about—what never enters your developing mind—is that one day, you and your eleven-year-old sister would be walking home from the bus stop, and a familiar face would disarm you with a smile, a kind word, and a question about his brand-new puppy, which got out.

Yeah, that happened.

"I let her out to go potty, but she ran off," the man who stopped us had said, scared. "I lost sight of her."

We helped him. Of course, we did, because... *it's a puppy!* But then a meaty hand clapped over my sister's mouth, her body went piano-wire tight, and her eyes bulged.

Yeah, that happened, too. For real.

My mouth fell open like an old mailbox with the lid down as this man, this monster, took my little sister's Barbie-blonde head and slammed it against the side of his van. The monster and I watched her fall unconscious to the ground and then our eyes met.

I bolted.

He charged after me.

When you're in this desperate, unimaginable situation, you think only of getting away and going for help. So, you do as I did: you take off like a shot. You do this while leaving your little sister behind because you can't do anything to help her; you can only help yourself and hope to get help for her, too. It breaks your heart to abandon her and makes you hate yourself for leaving, but what choice do you have? The reality was—and this entered my mind immediately—the monster meant for us *not to survive*.

Unfortunately, if you were a girl like me, your fourteen-year-old legs were still skinny and weak, and your knees were as knobby as your hips were bony, making it impossible to outrun a man his size.

You dash through the nearby meadow running full speed, as I did that fateful day, ignoring your quickening breath as it taxes your lungs and mixes with the hysteria circling like a tornado inside your head. Even though you're operating out of sheer terror, you can hear your beating heart, and it sounds like the *thump-thump-thump* of your feet pounding against the earth, grass, and wild daisies. You don't just run; you run your little heart out. Panic intensifies the scream building deep within you, a bloodcurdling wail you know will be so loud and bursting that when it finally explodes from your mouth it'll be shrill and full of sharp edges, and hopefully someone will hear you and rush to help.

Not far ahead lay a thicket of trees, possible salvation.

But it was too far away.

The scream became impossible to contain; it finally detonated, igniting like a bomb, expelling from me a savage, howling terror. The eruption was so powerful, so dizzying in its force, that I lost almost all my oxygen and nearly passed out. More screams followed, like aftershocks to an earthquake, or ripples in a pond.

Between the episodes of manic shrieking, I heard heavier feet than mine *clomp-clomp-clomping* behind me, beating the ground at a relentless pace. The anxiety of the chase was maddening, and I knew by the sounds that he'd closed the distance between us.

While I couldn't stop my boisterous hysteria, what made my skin crawl with goosebumps was the animalistic grunting sounds behind me, the terrifying noises that were too close and had gotten raspier and more hostile with every breath.

Tears streamed from my eyes, and my throat felt cheese-grater raw, and each cry for help now left a burning trail in its wake. While my anxiety and panic intensified, my speed did not. Nevertheless, I felt invisible hands inside my chest, squeezing the air from my lungs, trying to make me slow down and stop. If I stopped running, though, I knew I'd die.

So, I ran that day. I ran like my hair was on fire. I ran thinking only of my mean father and my drunk, absent-minded mother because I believed that if I could get to one or the other, everything would be okay. They would save me. And they would find a way to save my sister and make the evil man suffer.

But then a big, fleshy hand grabbed my brown hair, clutching the ponytail my mother had tied earlier that day. That morning, when the world was still okay, she told me that good girls went to school, steered clear of trouble, and studied hard so they could get good grades and not have a crap life with a mean man and degenerate kids. My mother, who smelled sour with sweat and boozy pores, said that as she gathered my loose hair and fashioned it into a haphazard ponytail. She then brushed the hair dutifully and methodically and used cheap hair wax to tame the frizzies and any flyaways. To this day, I don't blame her for not knowing what Natalie and I would endure in the days ahead, for she couldn't have known that her choice of hairstyle for me that day made it easier for the monster chasing me to catch me.

Before I realized I was no longer running free, that I was a caught fish, snagged by the hook that was his God-sized hand, the heaving brute jerked my ponytail so hard that my head stopped moving. Unfortunately, my body kept going. Suddenly, my legs were airborne in front of me, my body went horizontal to the ground, and I knew it was all over. The second my back slammed into packed earth I couldn't breathe. I was that fish pulled out of the water, beat against the side of a tree, and dropped into the dirt.

As I lay in the meadow grass writhing and gulping for air, this dying fish of a girl stared up at a ferocious creature, one who held my terrified gaze with cold, murderous eyes. I wanted to roll over, scramble to my feet, and take off running with every fiber of my being. My body would not respond, though—nothing worked the way it should.

Is he going to kill me now?

The brute towered over me, a giant with a heaving, barrel chest and big hands that made and unmade themselves into fists at a lunatic's pace. He wore crusty leather work boots with thick laces, old jeans he'd rubbed a hundred and a half dirty palms on, and a 70s-style white-and-blue-striped tee shirt with corn-colored stains in the armpits. His beard was heavy but wiry and unkempt. His lips were hideous and thin, and his nose was bulbous in size with more than a few visible blackheads, each bigger than a pinhead. A long rope of snot had escaped one cavernous nostril and was draped across his mustache.

He turned and spat on the ground, expelling a big breath that probably smelled foul, like rotting organs and cold, black coffee.

Snuggled on his head was a filthy trucker's hat with the patch of a red Chevy truck stitched onto the front. Below the Chevy, also sewn into the fabric, was the name of a local gas station. The bill was curved in a perfect arch and worked over the years like a catcher's mitt, making the hat look older than Natalie and me combined. He took it off, ran a hand over a head of thinning black hair, and then pulled the cap back on.

This terrifying freak show of a man drew a deeper breath, for he was winded like me. My chest finally loosened, and I found I could breathe again. Unfortunately, I started to hyper-ventilate.

The monster's cracked lips peeled back into a grin, but then he frowned, snorted like he was trying to suck in all the oxygen on earth, and spat another giant loogie. The second it struck my face, I turned away, humiliated.

"You little turd," he growled. "Making me run after you like that."

I wiped the thick snot and saliva into the dirt, then turned and glared up at him. He remained abnormally still, save for his heavy breathing and those cruel, inquisitive eyes. I refused to look away, if only because my father told me there was nothing in this world worse than a coward. The man's expression gave way to his amusement, but then he rolled his neck and right shoulder, getting pops out of each.

"Coulda twisted a knee, busted a hip, or fell over and broke a rib," he muttered, unblinking and no longer entertained.

He spat again, this time into the grass beside me, and then he looked around. I had no idea what to say because I couldn't stop thinking of Natalie. Was she okay or injured? Did she get away? My eyes zeroed in on him, loathing his white-trash looks, hating everything about him for what he was doing to us.

"I know you," my mouth finally said, the raspy words betraying any common sense I had left.

The chilling look of his eyes said plenty, enough for me to realize my error. Maybe things would've been different had I kept my damn mouth shut. But maybe not. Say what you want, killers don't want you seeing their faces, knowing their names, or even acknowledging them unless they were busy killing you at the time. I wasn't so wise back then, not by any measure, but even *I* knew dead girls tell no tales.

Aggressive growling coming from deep in his throat, he bent

and grabbed hold of my ankle, and then he turned and dragged me back through the field, returning to his van. I began screaming again but stopped when he spun around lightning quick. He dropped my leg in the dirt, then stood over the top of me in a frightening display of power. He bent low this time, bringing his face so close to mine that I could see every unsavory detail of it, including a pair of electric blue eyes.

Stabbing a hot-dog-sized finger at me, he said, "You scream one more time and I'm gonna snap your pencil neck in half. You got that, girl?"

Paralyzed and unable to breathe, I felt my bladder loosen. Wet warmth flooded my crotch, a dark stain spreading through my pants to the insides of my thighs. Soon, my skin was urine-soaked. I was too scared to feel shame and too small to offer an apology. Rather than tell the creep I wouldn't scream anymore, my head bobbed in a wordless, involuntary nod, one which seemed to satisfy him.

He narrowed his eyes as if checking me for signs of a lie, but with a snort of approval, he grabbed my ankle and resumed his trek, dragging me through grass and stickers, across dirt and tangles of weeds, and over a million little rocks. When I didn't think I could take the pain anymore, the monster quickened his pace like a madman on a mission, further intensifying my agony. I tried to keep quiet, but it was becoming impossible.

The back of my head bumped along the ground when I couldn't hold it up anymore, and my shirt had worked its way up my back, far enough for the ground to scratch and scrape my tender flesh. My mouth made mewling sounds and chirped tiny unintentional cries—I couldn't help it. I tried digging my palms into the earth in an attempt to lift my back off the dirt and stop the stinging pain. It was no use. The only thing I did was tear up my palms. Still, the urge to do *something* overwhelmed me. I wanted to kick the man, break free, and try to run. But he was a monster, and I was a stupid little girl.

When we finally reached his van, he threw my leg down into

the dirt and stood there, hands planted on his hips, his body slightly bent and out of breath. He scanned the surrounding lands for witnesses, then he stretched his back and took another look. Slowly, despite the pain, I turned on my side for a look of my own. Fresh tears boiled in my eyes, but I realized my sister was gone.

Natalie got away!

The monster, the beast, this inhuman atrocity, saw the same thing and roared inside his mouth like a freaking whack-a-doo. He spun around and glared at me. "Get up!"

Gingerly, I stood.

My big, frightened eyes watched his right hand become a fist at his side. These same helpless eyes watched his forearm muscles tense, and then I just stood there as he cocked that fist and held it like a loaded gun.

Yeah, I was dead.

Sometimes, the way you experience intense situations, how they're moving fast in reality but seem to slow in your brain, you stand there like a big, dumb animal, fixated on that one scary outcome, not even moving because fear turns you into a wax statue. That was me watching that fist heading straight for my face. I might have shut my eyes; if so, that was my only defense. The ham-sized bundle of bones collided with my head so hard I don't remember seeing or feeling anything after the initial shock, not until I woke up in a strange, twin-sized bed in some basement room that was cold, creepy, and stained in places with what I suspected was splattered blood.

I blinked to clear my vision, to let my eyes adjust to the low lighting, and then I shifted my body to test for injuries. I felt beat up and wrung out, but nothing was broken. When I finally came to, enough for my vision to sharpen, I saw several cameras set up on tripods all around me—video and photography, one camera with a big flashbulb attached and an umbrella-like contraption perched beside it.

I tried to sit up for a better look but got so dizzy that I

collapsed under a wave of intense agony, the edges of my vision going fuzzy before I fell over.

Did I black out? I think so...

When I opened my eyes again, most of the light was gone; only a bare overhead lightbulb glowed, casting the small space in weak amber hues while creating varying depths of shadows in the room's corners. I tried to get my head around this without panicking. But then I realized that someone else was here with me; I felt their presence. A shiver crawled up my spine, and I couldn't tear my eyes away from the darkest parts of the room.

Is the monster with me?

Oh, dear God, I thought I could hear him breathing.

I closed my eyes against my mind's chaotic thoughts, which was no easy feat, considering my head felt like someone ran over it with a pickup truck. I fought to contain the swell of emotion, and then I forced my eyes open, catching sight of my bare legs. *Where the hell are my pants, and why am I sitting in my underwear and bra?* Breathless, too scared to scream, I needed to know what was going on, yet having the answer terrified me.

Just sit up, I told myself.

Only then did I realize someone had bound my wrists and ankles with rope. I tested the bindings and found some play in them, but it was not enough to free myself from the bedposts to which each limb was tied. I pushed up into a V-shaped, seated position but coughed from the abrupt pressure around my neck. For a moment, I couldn't move. But then I grabbed what felt like a dog collar, followed the leather strap around to the back of my neck, and found the chain attached to it. Leaning forward to the point of discomfort allowed me to grab the chain with both hands, but a sturdy tug told me what I needed to know: I was now a prisoner.

A soft whimper escaped me as new levels of terror unfolded. I scooted up against the metal headboard as far as my various bindings would allow, easing the pressure off my throat. Looking around, I loathed the sight of everything I could see, yet I was more aware of all the things hiding that I had yet to see.

The room was smaller than I thought with low ceilings and no natural light source. Suddenly, I was struck with a certain sense of familiarity. *Had I been here before? No.* I understood immediately. The space resembled a movie set you might see at Nickelodeon or Disney studios if you were working behind the scenes on a scary movie.

While shadows concealed the room's deeper corners, potentially hiding things I couldn't see, a body lay curled on the floor, unconscious and chained to the wall. My little sister. My eyes prickled with tears; I blinked them away, wishing I could see her through moist eyes and the gloom. But I couldn't. It didn't matter, though, not the way her body lay perfectly still. *She's dead, I know it.* Had he beaten her to death?

Tears rolled down my cheeks and my shoulders trembled. *Dear God, please let her be alive.* I would have promised Him anything at that moment if He would help her take one big breath.

Without warning, something in the shadows stirred, a shifting darkness that flowed like a wave. The shadow of a man appeared, moving toward the large camera. A flash of light blinded me while the popping sound of a flashbulb made me flinch. Suddenly, unexpectedly, I was acutely aware of my body. I knew I was underdeveloped for a girl my age, and my bra was prematurely large and showed how slowly I was developing, but I did a good job hiding myself. Mostly. Well, until now. I crossed my knees, clamping them tightly to conceal my privates, and I tried to scrunch my shoulders together, but that pushed my bra cups wide open. I quickly relaxed my shoulders, but not my legs—another flash of light, another pop of sound. I glanced at my sister's dead body where she lay vulnerable, forgotten, and unable to move ever again.

Another *pop!*

The flash of light hurt my eyes, causing me to squint and turn away. This jerk took our clothes but left us our undergarments. I should have been thankful, but I wasn't. He should have never taken us in the first place.

Pop!

I tried to shield my eyes from the blinding light, which came from another camera this time, one much closer, one the creep used to follow my face every time I turned away.

Pop!

His presence was too close and overwhelming, yet the consecutive flashes kept me from seeing him as nothing more than a shadow. I hid my face and scooted away from him, but my hands, and the limitations caused by my restraints, could not prevent the strobe light flashes from stinging my brain.

"Stop!" I finally yelled.

The creature behind the camera rose to his full height and laughed—a low, mean chortle, like an old engine trying to start but having the hardest time.

"Desperate people pay good money for a dream like you. But mentally defective, *rich* people pay a whole lot more."

"Why are you doing this?" I asked, pleading.

"Money, of course, but fun, too."

"You're a pig!"

His low, soft laughter raked over me, making me feel sick to my stomach. "The world is full of people aching to see girls like you, little Sadie Gray," he whispered, his voice glazed with humor and hints of need. "Do you know how many people want to see you?"

The popping sounds and starbursts of light had stopped, so I lowered my guard and focused instead on the man behind the camera. He remained a shadow, but it was not so dark that I missed the minor details on his dog-ugly face and that vile, twisted smirk.

"Take a guess," he said.

"No."

My defiance failed to move him. "The answer is easy: we are but two tiny fish in an ocean of perverts. You can't see them, but they're there. Everywhere. They sell us our fast food, host community events you and your family attend, and run our schools, churches, and welfare centers—all with money to burn if the girl is right. And do you know what?"

"Be quiet!"

"Oh, Sadie Gray," he purred, clucking his tongue in delight, "they're gonna *love* you."

My chest tightened and I wondered if I was going to die. *Can fourteen-year-old girls have heart attacks?*

Pop!

I shielded my eyes again.

The man chuckled at my response, his voice that rusty V8 laugh—the slow, phlegmy giggle of a creep who liked to scare helpless girls.

"You should see your dumb face," he whispered while sounding pleased with himself. "I might even keep that picture for myself."

Pop!

In an unexpected fit, he stepped in and tore my hand away from my face, threw it down on the bed, and snapped more photos. When I began to cry, he grew unnaturally silent and took twice as many pictures. And when I lay down in defeat, resigned to my awful fate—whatever it was he had in store for me—the creep took a half-dozen more photos.

All I could do was cry.

"They pay a lot for the fear, the giving up, and the killing," the monster continued, taunting her. Then he tapped an old video camera where it sat on a tripod. "That's what this baby's for. You start doing them unforgivable things—things there ain't no coming back from—well, you film it with an eight-millimeter camera. It gets you that grainy look from the '70s and '80s. Folks pay extra for the effect, you know? The nostalgia and whatnot."

Until that moment, I wasn't sure about what he had in store

for me, but he'd just said it clear as day and I knew he meant it: he aimed to hurt me until I was dead.

Dead like my sister.

two
earl "mop up" gray

THE MINUTE EARL got home from work he sensed something was wrong. The first indication came when he saw the empty front yard. The girls were usually swinging together on the swing set, bouncing on the trampoline, running around the yard, or playing one outdoor made-up game or another.

"Hello!" he called to his girls and wife.

He walked through the vacant house, hearing only an echo. Through the kitchen, on the other side of the large picture windows, out on the porch talking on the phone, he found Gabriella. The intense expression on her face stopped him. Who was she speaking to like that? She glanced up, saw him, and froze.

Earl felt his nostrils flare as he drew a deep breath. What did he interrupt? While he didn't want to think about her talking to another man, considering how unhappy she was with him and their life, it was entirely possible.

She glanced away quickly, ignoring him. *Okay...* He watched her for a moment longer, his heart taking off at a sprint, and he thought of everything he would do to any guy trying to get with her. But then she turned, and their eyes met again. Despite their recent difficulties, Earl faced the sudden possibility that it wasn't about another man.

Earl crossed through the kitchen, opened the slider and screen door, and took the phone from his wife.

"Who is this?"

"Mr. Gray?" the female voice asked.

Okay, he didn't expect that. He returned the phone to Gabriela, satisfied at having heard a woman's voice rather than some man's. Embarrassed but not making a big deal of it, Gabby took the phone, apologized for Earl's behavior, thanked the woman, and ended the call.

"I'm sorry," he said, even though he wasn't sorry.

Rather than speak to him, she collapsed into his arms, her body trembling, tears glistening in her eyes.

"Gabby?" he pulled back and asked.

"They didn't come home," she said, pulling him closer and sniffling as she spoke into his shirt.

The four words spoken together had an immediate effect. Earl held her for a moment, just long enough to process the news, and then he gently stepped back to an arm's length and gripped her shoulders. Looking deeply into her eyes, reminding himself to remain calm, he said, "Tell me everything you know. Leave nothing out."

Gabby told him they never came home, so she called Carol, the school administrator. "That was who I was talking to," she said, recalling the conversation. Again, she was overcome with emotion.

He drew a deep breath, trying to stay calm, but he felt the fear creeping in. "Do you think something bad happened to them?"

She swallowed hard and nodded.

"Okay, then," he whispered.

If Earl was going to find them, if they were lost or gone or terrible things happened, he faced the possibility that he could no longer be Earl Gray—the decent father and passable husband, the warm cup of tea of a man in front of others. If someone hurt them, or... or... *no,* he couldn't let himself go there. If he did, he would have to become someone different, someone mean and determined, the kind of hunter that polite society needed but abhorred. He would have to be Earl "Mop Up" Gray, the former CIA officer who worked dirty, with ruthless efficiency and a cold, uncaring heart. Mop Up had done the kinds of vile things other men couldn't or wouldn't do, even when no one was looking.

Gabby had burned herself on the hot edges of this man a time or two, and shades of him appeared when least expected, but Gabby and the girls had no idea who he truly was when the mask came off, what he was capable of doing, or the dark, nasty secrets he harbored. If Earl Gray couldn't figure this out, Mop Up was coming sooner rather than later.

Gabby wiped her eyes and cleared her throat. "Carol said one of the teachers watched them get on the bus and leave, but no one knows more than that."

"Can we talk to the bus driver?"

"She said she'd reach out, which was why I thanked her."

He remained silent, grinding his molars.

"I called Martha Matheson up the street—you can see the bus stop from her living room window," Gabby added. "But she said she's been on the can all afternoon on account of an extra-spicy chili Fred cooked up last night."

He pinched his nose together, not wanting that visual.

"I also called Coach Tilly. He said he was napping and hadn't seen Sadie or Natalie but would help if needed."

Earl checked his watch and noted the time. "So, they've been missing about two hours, then?"

Gabby nodded, tears bubbling in her eyes, her lips pinched together as if she was barely hanging on.

He drew her into another hug, told her it would be okay, and said, "Give me the phone. Let me see what I can do."

He called Grass Valley PD and asked to speak to the police chief directly. The operator directed him to Skip Davenport's line; it rang five times and went to voicemail. He left a message.

"Hey, Skip, it's Earl Gray here. My girls didn't come home from school today. They got on the bus, but no one has seen them since. We've been calling friends and neighbors but are coming up empty-handed. Please call back as soon as—"

The call-waiting feature beeped softly. Earl glanced at the phone's screen and saw it was Chief Davenport; he switched lines and took the call.

"Skip, thanks for calling back."

"You bet, Earl, what can I do you for?" he asked in a friendly tone.

Earl explained the situation in as much detail as he could.

Skip let out a long, low sigh. "Any chance they got distracted with something, a friend or whatnot? You know girls their age—scatterbrained and carefree."

"My girls always come home, Skip."

Skip exhaled audibly, seemed to think about it, and asked, "How far is the bus stop from your place?"

"Quarter-mile, give or take."

"I think I've got an officer I can send your way," he replied, as if mentally combing his roster for someone. "I'm gonna holler at her now. Her partner is out on paternity leave, so it'll just be her."

"That's fine," Earl said.

"See if you can round up a few neighbors and start searching that quarter-mile between the bus stop and your place."

Trying to sound grateful, Earl said, "Thanks for your help, Skip."

"No problem. Don't worry, we'll find them."

Earl's mind took a different turn, giving him a moment's pause. Then, he said, "I wish I didn't have to worry, but then I start thinking of Mandy Coontz and Stella Rodriguez."

A prolonged bout of silence stretched over the airways between them. "That ain't the same thing, Earl."

"You guys never found them, did you?"

"You know about our staffing shortage, the realignment of priorities, and the budget cuts that have hit us all, right?"

"I heard something on the news, but..."

Beside him, Gabby started to weep; she turned and sobbed,

trying hard to control herself. Earl chastised himself for speaking the missing girls' names aloud. He should have known better, but he was as scared as she was, maybe more.

"Those cases went cold," Skip said matter-of-factly.

"Both?"

"Uh-huh, yeah. For now."

Gabby collapsed into one of the patio recliners, pulled her legs to her chest, and dropped her forehead onto her knees. Earl watched her body shake. It was only a matter of time before she went for the vodka or wine to take off the edge.

Earl returned to the house and closed the slider behind him. "More than just Mandy and Stella went missing, Skip. Four girls, if I recall correctly."

"Six if you go back five years," Skip added without hesitation. "But that's just between you and me because I don't want to blow smoke up anyone's ass here."

Earl nodded, hating those stats. An unexpected rush of fear hit him like a slap. He took a deep breath, backed himself off that cliff, and quietly said, "You ever call it a serial, Skip?" *As in serial killer.*

"Internally, yeah. But not to the press or public. I expect you to keep it that way, considering our history and the sensitivities of those affected."

Earl made a fist and wanted to punch something. Instead, he relaxed his hand and ran it through his hair, felt the rowdier parts of him trying to resurface, and didn't wholly object. Skip knew him, though. Before he was Chief Davenport, he was in the Army, where they served together.

Earl finally said, "Earl Gray is nice, *a good guy,* but if we don't find my girls by their bedtime, you're going to get Mop Up."

Skip processed the bold, almost threatening statement in complete silence, and then he said, "Please don't do that, Earl. You know that's not good for anyone."

"It'll be good for my girls if that's what it takes to find them."

"Let's not wind ourselves up over a bunch of 'what-if'

scenarios before we've even started looking," he said with an authoritative air of finality. "Gather your neighbors as I suggested earlier, and I'll send Officer Teresa May to assist. Let's conserve our energy for finding them girls."

Skip was right, but that was why he was the police chief and not some guy who ran side jobs to eke out a meager living for a family of four, which had become Earl's lot in life.

"Let the system work for you, Earl," Skip reassured him. "Trust me."

"Okay," he said reluctantly.

When Gabby saw Earl end the call, she stood and walked inside. "Please don't repeat their names," she said softly.

He drudged up an apologetic look. "I should've thought better 'for I spoke."

"You should have, yes, but I understand," Gabby mumbled.

"It's time to find the girls."

"Where do we start?"

Earl turned the situation over in his head and spooled up plans, knowing that if he couldn't find the girls quickly, he would cede control to Mop Up despite Skip's pointed request. With Skip knowing Earl the way he did, he was right to ask him not to be that guy.

But Sadie and Natalie were his and Gabby's life, and without them, the delicate balance he maintained at home and in life would surely unravel into the kind of hellscape even he wouldn't let himself imagine.

three
officer teresa may

TWENTY-EIGHT-YEAR-OLD TERESA MAY sat with her friend, Lacy, at a table in Lumberjack's, a quaint country café off Nevada City Highway in Brunswick Basin, almost halfway between Nevada City and Grass Valley. The food was good, and the atmosphere was comfortable. It was made even cozier by the polished wood floors, half-log walls, and log chairs with comfortable, forest-green cushions. Locals knew the Lumberjack as a sit-down restaurant where you could order whatever you wanted no matter the time of day, and no one would get rubbed the wrong way.

Looking across the table at Lacy, who was not a happy girl, Teresa said, "Get it out, girl. Just say it."

"It's so embarrassing, though," Lacy whispered.

By then, their food had arrived. Lacy had ordered turkey and potatoes, and Teresa had her favorite sandwich—The Chain Saw. The roast beef sandwich had bacon, tomatoes, sautéed onions and mushrooms, bell peppers, cheddar cheese, and a special dressing, all smashed together on grilled sourdough toast.

She joked with her old partner (currently on paternity leave) that half the extra twenty pounds she'd gained since joining Grass Valley PD came from The Chain Saw.

"I caught him looking at pornos," Lacy swallowed, her eyes

red and starting to glisten. She said that like it was her last breath and only chance to speak. Then she stuffed too much turkey and potatoes into her mouth and started chewing like a twelve-year-old.

"So, your new boyfriend was looking at some stuff?" Teresa asked, careful not to be too dismissive of her feelings. "That's like saying you caught him drinking beer or eating Funyuns on the crapper."

Lacy stopped chewing her turkey, refused to swallow, and mumbled, "Ain't the same thing and you know it." Some turkey bits fell out of her mouth.

"It kinda sorta is, Lacy," she said, watching her friend gulp half her soda to force down the turkey. "Guys like girls, no mystery there. And the only thing better than seeing their girl is seeing five-hundred-thousand girls online whenever they want. We're a changed society, my friend—welcome to the dating apocalypse."

Lacy finished swallowing but did so while quietly crying. Then she ate more, sniffled more, and half-swallowed enough food that she had to guzzle half her soda to force it over the lump in her throat—poor thing.

Teresa discreetly glanced outside, eying her police cruiser where it sat in the parking lot. How long until lunch would get interrupted by a call? She didn't expect it, but anything was possible. Lunch with Lacy was precious, something neither friend did together often, so she hoped they could finish their meals without interruption.

Lacy changed pace, chewing her food too slowly while wiping her eyes. When she looked across the table at Teresa, it was with heavy eyes. "You don't understand."

Working in law enforcement had hardened the softer side of her personality, and Teresa was not unsympathetic to the situation. But she was there to offer support, not cast judgment. If only she were a warmer person, a more understanding friend.

Her luck with men was for crap, though, same as Lacy. They had become their own support group.

"Maybe you could explain it to me," Teresa said before taking another big bite of her sandwich.

Lacy swallowed a mouth full of slowly-chewed food and wiped her eyes again. Then her expression suddenly changed, losing its sorrowful look, and her features hardened with the recollection of another painful memory. "He was looking at videos with *guys* in them."

Just guys, or guys in videos with girls? "It takes two to tango when a girl wants some proper loving from a man," Teresa said, becoming increasingly uncomfortable with the turn of events.

"*All* guys," Lacy clarified with stern conviction. Her eyes were drier than the Gobi Desert, her pain now replaced by outrage.

Teresa stopped chewing and glanced up at her friend; it was as if Lacy had been staring at her for a hundred years without blinking.

Slowly, Teresa said, "Yeah, that's a problem."

Lacy narrowed her eyes, satisfied that she finally got it. Then she went back to pushing her food around the plate with her fork, her eyes vacant. Without looking up, she asked, "You think that's why he stopped being intimate?"

Teresa laughed before catching herself, and she damn near choked on her food while trying to take it back. She told herself to be decent, then took a deep, contemplative breath, held Lacy's lost eyes with her empathetic gaze, and said, "I'm gonna say 'yes' on this, and it ain't much of a stretch."

"We were in love, though," Lacy whispered, her façade cracking again.

Teresa reached out and took her friend's hand, holding it to reassure her she was not alone, that she was okay, and that she had friends to lean on. Then she said, "You're a beard, sweetheart."

"I have a what?" Lacy asked, withdrawing her hands to touch her face.

"No, stop touching your face," Teresa said. "You don't *have* a beard; you *are* a beard. A beard is a woman a gay guy keeps around to maintain the air of heterosexuality."

Before she could say more, Avery Lee, GVPD's dispatcher, reached out to her. "Hold that terrible thought," Teresa said. She keyed her mic. "Say again, over?"

Avery repeated the call: "Two missing girls in Birchwood Meadow Acres, just off Rattlesnake Road at Oak Ridge."

"Ages?" she asked, a sick feeling forming in her gut.

"It's Earl Gray's girls," he said softly, reverently. "Sadie and Natalie."

She felt a cold wave of horror wash over her. A while back, Nevada City PD picked Earl up on a drunk and disorderly complaint at the Mine Shaft Saloon, then tried to charge him with seven counts of felony assault when they saw he'd torn through a rowdy pack of bikers. It turned out to be self-defense, according to one bartender, a friend of Teresa, who said the bikers started it and Earl was forced to finish it. Nevertheless, the Mine Shaft Saloon's staff swept up smashed bottles, overturned chairs, broken teeth, and a few pulled chunks of hair. After that, it took just over an hour to mop up all the blood.

Some people in the department and around town said Earl escaped justice because he was friends with Chief Davenport, but Teresa had seen the surveillance video and knew to steer clear of the man. Drinking or not, the few times she encountered him, he looked like a powder keg ready to blow.

"Does the chief know about this, over?" Teresa asked dispatch reverently.

"He requested you, over. Code three." *Lights and sirens.*

"Roger that."

"Earl will meet you at the corner of Rattlesnake and Oak Ridge Drive. Set up a search grid. Use what daylight you have left to your advantage. Those are the chief's words, not mine. We need to find those little girls before dusk."

"I'm on my way now," she said.

"What's your 20?"

"I'm sitting down at Lumberjack's, having lunch with a friend."

"Oh, no," Avery said, his voice almost too soft for transmission. "You're not eating The Chain Saw, are you?"

"Roger that," she said, embarrassed.

"You know what happened to you last time..."

"Can't talk now," she interrupted him to say, "I'm lights and sirens after I doggie bag it and settle up."

"Chief wants a status report ASAP," Avery said. "I'll tell him you're on your way in five, over."

"10-4, I'll report on the scene."

She looked across the table at Lacy, who had sobered up having heard the news. "Your dispatcher sounds cute."

"He's not," she replied. "Avery's old and not even a sworn officer."

"Did he say the father's name is 'Earl Gray'?"

She nodded and flagged their server.

"Like the tea?"

"But not sweet," Teresa said.

"Oh."

"Keep this on the down-low, please."

"I will," Lacy said.

The last thing the city needed was another missing girl. What it needed less was an unpredictable father like Earl Gray turning into a psychopathic wrecking ball. All seven men from the bar fight at the Mine Shaft Saloon spent time in Sierra Nevada Memorial Hospital; one had his jaw wired shut for six weeks, and to this day, he still couldn't talk right.

When their server arrived, Teresa asked for a doggie bag. The woman nodded, knowing the drill. Response times were critical to maintaining confidence in the local police, something Chief Davenport drilled into everyone's heads.

She placed a twenty-dollar bill on the table and said, "Find a decent guy who likes girls; he'll fall in love with you."

"You say that now," Lacy said, trying to smile.

"You have a beautiful face, sweetie. And every guy I know talks about your butt in jeans like it's the second coming of Christ or something," Teresa grinned. "Go with it. You won't be single for more than a week or two."

"What about Les?" Lacy asked.

"Leave his stuff on the front lawn, but don't burn it."

Lacy laughed bitterly, then said, "I'll call you if he gets fussy."

Their server brought her a to-go bag, which she stuffed with the rest of her sandwich. She then stood and hugged her friend. "Love you, Lacy."

"Love you, too, Teresa. Thank you."

Teresa smiled again, then headed outside, climbed into her cruiser, and pulled out onto the highway. She accelerated to twenty miles over the posted speed limit, flipping on her lights and siren in the process.

She was on the scene in no time flat where she saw Earl Gray talking to what looked like a small search party of folks you'd never see at upscale restaurants or the gym. Teresa was happy to have these folks; no one worked harder to find local kids than the redneck search parties, something she had come to love about these smaller, family-oriented communities.

She contacted dispatch with a 10-23, meaning she'd arrived on the scene, then exited the car and scanned the many faces. There must be two dozen people. What dialed her blood pressure back was seeing the old high school coach standing in the mix. Guys who ran football teams could lead on search parties well. It looked like Coach Tilly was talking with Earl, and Earl was nodding in agreement.

Earl Gray saw the cruiser, excused himself, and made a beeline for her, thanking her immediately for coming to help.

"We're about to fan out," he said, skipping the chit-chat. "Coach will fill you in, but we've got limited daylight, and the woods around here can be pretty thick. We have to use what light we have before we start bumping into trees."

Teresa nodded and said, "We'll find them, Mr. Gray. It's probably a case of falling or hurting themselves or losing track of time."

If they could find them before dusk, she wouldn't have to spend tomorrow knocking on doors. In this deeply rural neighborhood, Teresa wasn't sure if she'd be savaged by attack dogs, harassed by bad-tempered residents defending their privacy, or shot by growers if she found herself wandering onto weed-producing property on which she had no business.

Earl stared at her briefly, narrowed his eyes, and then smacked his lips as if he didn't like what she said. "Less talking, more walking," he said before turning to the volunteers and saying, "We're heading down Oak Meadows Road toward Round Tuit Road!"

"Yeah," Teresa muttered to herself. "Roger that."

"He's just scared," Coach Tilly said, surprising her. He'd come up on her side and didn't seem to realize her tunnel vision for Earl. "We're *all* scared on account'a them other missing girls."

"Don't mention them right now, please," Teresa said, straightening her back. Coach seemed to understand. He didn't seem book smart, nor did he look it, but she trusted him to be helpful.

Nodding solemnly, the coach said. "'Course not, Officer." He knocked his head with the tips of his fingers and frowned. "What was I thinking?"

"As Earl said, 'Less talking, more walking,'" Teresa replied as she breezed past him to take half the search party and split up to cover more ground. "Let's go."

Everything was fine until she saw Sewer Jones. The fifteen-year-old kid was a scrub if she'd ever seen one, and he wasn't intimidated by the police, considering he'd spent time in Nevada County Juvenile Hall last year.

"Look at you, fine as ever," he said to Teresa like a punk. He leaned his head back, stroked his chin, and grinned. His mother, Ethel, smacked the back of his head so hard he stumbled forward.

"Knock it off, Stuart," she barked. Ethel Jones was a big woman, so large that all she wore were house dresses and busted flats for shoes.

About five months back, Stuart Jones, a.k.a. Sewer Jones, was trying to set off illegal fireworks in the sewer system. He said he wanted to "blow shit up" when cops found him. All that happened was an illegal M-80 went off and covered him in raw sewage. From that day on, Stuart Jones was only Stuart to his mother; to everyone else, he was Sewer Jones.

"Is he coming with us?" Teresa snapped, pointing at Sewer.

Ethel nodded. "He's a good boy, just misunderstood."

"If he shuts his mouth and follows our lead, there will be no misunderstanding," Teresa said. "Am I making myself clear, young man?"

"You're, like, only a few years older than me," Sewer said, grinning at first before tempering his smile. He looked sideways at his mother, who glared at him as if trying to set his soul ablaze.

"I'm twice your age, Son. Do what your mommy says, and don't make any trouble."

"Yes, Ma'am," Sewer mumbled.

By Teresa's watch, they had three hours of daylight, at best, while only two hours remained in her shift. She'd be lucky to get home before dawn.

"All right," Teresa announced to her part of the search party. "Until someone can round up a chopper, we will conduct an official ground search. Check anywhere someone might hide and anywhere someone might hide someone else. Follow my lead, and let's keep a tight, clean line." All eyes were on her, each filled with determination to find the girls, even Sewer.

Teresa led her volunteers down Oak Ridge Drive, immediately passing a single-story home with an '80s look, complete with tan siding, faded maroon-colored trim, and a two-door junker parked out front. The eleven of them cut through the front yard, walking over mowed weeds and past a trimmed pine tree, making their way into the middle of the paved asphalt road: Oak Meadows Drive.

From there, they fanned out into the woods and open properties, calling the girls' names as they made their way to the split ahead. While Oak Meadows veered right, a new road, Round Tuit Road, continued and ran parallel to Oak Meadows. Earl said he'd take Round Tuit while Teresa and her team followed Oak Meadows.

"Sadie!" Teresa called as she climbed a small dirt embankment covered with pine needles and loose soil. Atop the small hill stood a thicket of pine trees. "Natalie, Sadie!"

Beside her, Sewer called out the girls' names. His proximity startled her, but he didn't seem to notice. He had managed to catch up to her and kept her pace.

The party's calls echoed down the line, and just when Teresa warmed up her knees and found her rhythm, her stomach let out a long, burly growl, one so noisy that she quickly covered her belly with a hand.

"Oh, my God, did you just pass gas?" Sewer asked next to her.

four
sadie gray

THE MONSTER LEFT the basement and tromped up the creaky wooden staircase. Before leaving, he snapped off the single overhead bulb, plunging my dead sister and me into darkness. My eyes needed a minute to adjust to the darkness, but it was so dark the world felt like an ocean of ink. I couldn't even see my hand in front of my face!

On the ceiling above, at what I assume was the home's main level, loose boards and weak joints flexed and squealed ever so slightly. I focused on the sounds enough to know the creep was walking around by himself, casual as a Sunday afternoon—as if he hadn't done a darn thing wrong to Natalie and me. But then, a second set of footsteps entered the picture, this person walking much lighter than our abductor.

While my mind invented numerous possibilities, each worse than the last, I went to work testing my binds, pulling on the chain against my collar and the wall, and trying frantically to wiggle my wrists out of the ropes attached to the bedposts. After ten minutes of exhausting myself and getting nowhere, the only thing I accomplished was to put a massive dent in my optimism. Discouraged, I flopped down on the dirty bed and started to cry, wishing my sister was still alive.

"Is he gone?" the tiniest of voices whispered.

Breathless, practically rendered mute, I tried to make sense of the voice while my heart raced a million miles an hour with the possibility that she was still alive. *Could it be...?*

"I think," I replied with a croak.

I was fixin' to ask who said that when the same small voice said, "He likes to take pictures when you're crying. If you pretend to be dead, he'll take less pictures."

I pushed myself to the side of the bed as far my binds would allow and said, "Natalie? Is that you?" I was desperate to believe it was her, but what if it wasn't? What if it was another girl like me lured here by talk of puppies and violence? As much as my hope was soaring, hope can lift you or crush your spirits entirely.

"I don't hear him no more," Natalie whispered, speaking a little louder.

"I thought you were dead," I said, tears pooling in my eyes.

"You know I can hold my breath longer than you, right?" Natalie asked—a statement rather than a question. "Done it a million times in the pickle pools."

Of course, she could. Our father bought us two fifty-five-gallon pickle barrels we filled with hose water and kept in the back near the chicken coop. The coop in mid-summer was probably the worst thing I've ever smelled, but Natalie and I could deal with it because we had those big, plastic pickle pools for relief.

"You faked me out," I said, practically weeping. "I was sure he killed you."

"Almost faked myself out," Natalie replied softly.

I heard her sit up and scoot across the floor, moving toward me until the bindings caught. Then she took a breath and said, "He didn't kill me yet, but he's gonna kill us both, Sadie."

The darkness was thicker than molasses, making it hard to breathe. On the one hand, it felt like there was so much space around me I could fly to the moon, but then I knew where I was and started to feel claustrophobic. I only wanted to look at my sister, to know that my brain wasn't telling lies to mess with my heart. Squinting harder than before, I ached to see her, but all I saw was her shadow—another dark outline against a background just as black as everything else.

"Natalie?" I asked.

"Yeah."

"For real, is that you? You're not someone else playing games?"

"It's me, for real," she replied.

Relief finally washed over me, renewing my will to shed these restraints and get us both out of here, wherever "here" was. Unfortunately, no matter my efforts, the restraints remained intact. I lay back down again and told myself to think hard and find a way out. While I expected the tears to come rolling, my eyes had dried out because something in me had changed: I didn't want to cry anymore, not when considering the need to escape.

"If we don't get out of here, he's gonna kill us for real," Natalie said. Any relief I felt knowing my sister was alive felt short-lived.

The eleven-year-old was wise for her age and just as innovative as me in most ways, but she had a knack for calling things as they were. Where I possessed what my father called "discretion," my little sister had "candor." Our mother hated Natalie's candor and often lectured her on the virtue of having manners, common sense, and prudence. Those conversations were one-sided and seemed to have no lasting effect on Natalie. The girl had no filter. My dad said it all the time, and he wasn't wrong. Of course, I never felt she needed tempering because I've always appreciated my sister's outspokenness. More often than not, she was saying what I was thinking.

"Why did he do this to us?" I heard myself ask.

Before Natalie could answer, I thought of the bed I was in and who else might have been in this same predicament, bound to the frame the same as me. A hard chill raced down my spine, causing my skin to break into gooseflesh. I wanted to crawl under the thin blankets, having been hit with a subsequent shiver, but there was no telling what went on in this bed or underneath these blankets.

A second shiver hit, which resulted from the terrible things I could not stop thinking. If I wasn't tied to the bedposts and chose to slide under the blankets—if I felt something flaky scrape my skin—I would know right away it was someone else's dried blood.

Natalie quietly replied, "He took a crap ton of pictures. Then said we're lucky that the customers like us clothed before they like us... otherwise."

I lay so still I could be paralyzed. Then, with a surprised gasp, I asked, "Clothed?"

"He said it won't be that way when he starts shootin' videos."

A well of emotion boiled up from within me, followed by a cramping sensation in my stomach that hurt the rest of me. Think of a boa constrictor slithering around my guts, squeezing everything at once.

"Videos?" I heard myself ask, echoing Natalie's last word.

"I asked about the dried blood while you were unconscious," she said, continuing to speak quickly but in hushed tones. "Were you faking it, being unconscious?"

"No," I answered honestly. "I was unconscious."

"He said first there's pictures, then there's the videos, and then there's all the screaming for help, and bawling, and blood. He said most of the blood cleans up, but some of it gets left over for..."

Natalie stopped speaking, either because she couldn't say the word or because she had forgotten what the monster had said.

"For what?" I asked breathlessly.

A moment later, she answered. "Atmosphere—he said *atmosphere*. Does that mean like 'outer space'?"

"It means the mood of the room."

"Oh," she said.

I fought a debilitating surge of terror—a wave so overwhelming I either had to scream my head off or quietly roll over and accept my fate. If the monster intended to kill us, I prayed he would be quick. But we knew him. He wouldn't kill us, would he? He couldn't, *because we knew him... he knew us.*

"We have to get out of here," I finally said, speaking with enough conviction to jumpstart the fighter in me. As a big sister, it was up to me to save us both. That's how I had to think of it; so that's how it would be.

"He said we can get out," Natalie said, defeated, "only we can't do it while being alive. He's talking about us being dead, right? Because that's how it sounded when he said it. And that's why I said he was gonna kill us, for real."

"He's making snuff films," I heard myself say, having realized the things kids talked about at school sounded fantastic until you were stuck in some psychopath's basement waiting for him to slaughter you on film.

We heard a door open at the top of the stairs. We became as silent as church mice, but my eyes were keen, my senses aware of everything. A long shadow stretched down the wooden staircase and onto the basement floor—the shadow of a man or boy, or perhaps a butch woman.

"Shhh," the voice hissed from above.

How in Jesus' name were we supposed to be quiet under these conditions? "Can you please help us?" I asked, just loud enough to be heard.

The shadow remained—unmoving and unspeaking as if frozen in sudden contemplation. But then, the same shadow shrank back, closed and latched the door, and once again left us drowning in the darkness of our despair.

five
earl "mop up" gray

EARL AND A HOST of volunteers tramped through the dense forest, moving in an orderly fashion through heavy shrub at times, then across packed soil matted with pine needles, and even once across a small brook and several larger embankments.

"We need a dog," Earl grumbled at one point during the pitch-black night when he and Officer May met up.

"Right now, these nice folks and I are all you have, but the Sheriff likes you, so I figure if we come up short here tonight, he'll find a way to allocate further resources for the search."

Officer Teresa May was not an ugly woman, nor was she fit or fat, but she was a trooper, and Earl appreciated that she was still in the search; her steadfastness and Gabby's efforts to keep everyone hydrated and with snacks kept everyone else going.

"How come these girls keep going missing, and you can't find nothin' about them?" Coach Tilly finally approached her and asked.

Coach Tilly was Earl's neighbor. The older man was a legendary football coach known for good plays, an even temper, and his willingness to dig in when times were tough. However, his timing had waned in his advancing years, and he was now slightly off the mark.

"This isn't the place, Coach," Officer May said without

looking at him. She looked a bit winded and said her stomach was giving her grief.

"We're all thinking it," one of the other volunteers said.

Earl found himself nodding along.

"Doesn't mean y'all have to bring it up," Officer May quipped. "Besides, you'll scare Mrs. Gray if you speak of that around her."

"Too late," Earl grumbled.

Coach scratched behind his big ears and said, "I try not to be upset about it, but the fact that this... *monster*... ain't been caught yet, that them girls are still out there... *not found*. It's unsettling, and I, for one, think someone should address it."

"The leads went cold, Coach," Officer May finally spat. "What do you want me to say? The truth sucks for us all, but you don't want to hear that, and I'm not about to lie."

Coach studied her a long time, then said, "Sorry I brought it up."

"I'm not, despite Officer May's good points," Earl said, deadpan. "I can tell you this: if the same person who took them girls—if that's what that was—if he took my girls, I'll move heaven and earth to find him and unleash a lifetime of hell upon him."

Officer May ignored whatever gastrointestinal discomfort she might be feeling to stand up straight and level Earl with a look.

"What?" he asked. "You feel differently?"

"No, but I wear a badge, and we have a way of doing things lawfully."

"Maybe GVPD doing everything by the book kept this guy off the radar," Coach said. Then he threw his hands up and shook his head. "I shouldn't say no more about it. I won't. But it's off our chests now, so let's get back lookin' because them girls are out here somewhere."

"I'm glad you're here, Coach," Earl said, clapping a hand on his shoulder.

Coach nodded along with Officer May and a few others. But inside, Earl felt his cool veneer cracking. He knew that teachers, coaches, and school administrators all showed heart and compassion when it came to kids, so maybe he could lean on more of them and create a network of informants, so to speak.

Where Earl dared not voice his opinion about the department's efforts to find the girls, or failed efforts as it were, Coach had come to the rescue. Officer May seemed worried he would upset the others, but Earl and Coach knew it would only rally the troops through the midnight hour and into the cold morning light.

When the others split off and it was just him and Officer May, Earl looked at her and said, "I didn't think you'd last."

"The bad reputation our department has garnered over the missing girls keeps me working, Mr. Gray. First and foremost, we need to find your girls, but if this goes on longer than expected, I don't want anyone saying we didn't try, we gave up, and more girls went missing."

"You won't hear it from me if you keep on like this."

"We'll find them, Sir."

There was a handful of missing girls unaccounted for over the last few years, which turned so much of the public against the local PD that even the Nevada County Sheriff's Department whispered about their inability to keep the community safe.

Earl was about to tell Officer May he was ready to get after it again when what looked like a pinch of pain appeared to nip her deep in the gut, judging by her reaction.

She tried to hide her discomfort enough to say, "Let's focus on finding these girls now. They need you and Gabby."

"And the GVPD needs a win."

"Yes, indeed."

For the tenth time that night, or more, Earl wondered if his girls had fallen victim to a serial killer. It wasn't an unreasonable thought since, last he'd heard, somewhere between twenty and fifty serial killers were active across the nation at any given time. With California taking first place and nearly doubling the next state, Texas, in active serial killers, the thought was not one to dismiss.

"Is the department still focused on finding the other girls?" Earl heard himself ask when he saw Officer May's pain had passed. He smacked his neck, crushing a mosquito, but not before it got him. He was getting tired of being eaten by bugs.

He had posed the question, but suddenly, he didn't want an answer. Coach was right—they shouldn't be talking about this and he was sorry it got brought up. Then again, how hard was law enforcement trying to find these girls now that the hoopla around their disappearances had waned?

"Of course, we're still focusing on that," Officer May replied halfheartedly. She sneaked out a light burp, excused herself, and tried to look embarrassed.

Earl shook his head as he pushed through walls of fatigue, stress, and sorrow. He tried to settle his mind, telling himself they would find Sadie and Natalie and that everything would be okay. But if his girls were truly gone, then it would *not be* okay; nothing would ever be okay.

"I'll widen the search grid farther to your right," Officer May squeaked.

"I'll do it with her," one of the kids said, the little scrub they called "Sewer."

Officer May looked at the kid and frowned.

As far as Earl could recall, the Jones boy wasn't a model citizen, but he was a pair of eyes, which he'd take right now. Hell, he'd take whatever he could get.

Gazing down the line of folks with their flashlights and weary bodies in big jackets and hiking boots, he saw maybe twenty in all, each seemingly ready to return to the search. He finally pushed forward and heard the others follow.

"Sadie, Natalie!" he called.

Others returned to calling the girls' names, too. Just before he split off from Officer May, he thought he heard the Jones boy say, "Thatcher belly makin' all that noise, Officer?"

"Be quiet," Officer May might have mumbled. Then, clear as day, he heard what she said next, and her condition made sense. "I had a sandwich this afternoon and had to rush through most of it on account of Sadie and Natalie coming up missing."

Before the dumb kid could reply, Officer May called his girls' names; Sewer called their names now, too. But he couldn't leave well enough alone.

"What kinda sandwich?" he asked.

"Mind your own business, kid," Earl barked, still able to hear most of the conversation. "Can't you tell she don't want to talk to you? Focus, dammit. Focus!"

"Yes, Sir," he said, embarrassed.

Earl glanced sideways at Officer May and wondered how well she'd fare in a fight. "Sadie, Natalie!"

Their paths through the trees veered apart but converged once more, bringing him into proximity to Officer May and Sewer, close enough that he heard Officer May's stomach let out another long growl, one not even tromping through the woods could hide.

"Whatever sandwich you ate is doing backflips in your gut," Sewer said.

"It's from Lumberjacks," Officer May admitted.

"Which one?" Sewer asked.

Earl turned and looked at her as she slowed down, folded forward a touch, and held her stomach. "You okay, Officer May?" he asked.

She nodded, stood to her full height, and pressed on. "I'm all good, thanks."

Earl called the girl's names, then looked at her again.

She rolled her eyes and said, "It was a sandwich called 'The Chain Saw.'"

"You need to stop for a crap?" Sewer asked.

She scoffed, shook her head, and looked at Earl. "Can you believe the balls on this kid?"

"What about my nuts?"

"Dammit, Sewer!" Earl snapped.

"For the love of God, Sewer, I'm fine," Officer May said, motioning for Earl to calm back down. "Just mind your own business, or you can switch teams and walk with Earl."

"It's Stuart."

"It's Sewer to me and Earl so long as you're engaging in that third-grade bullshit talk about farts and crap. You know you're being rude, right? That you don't talk to women like that?"

"We're all human," Sewer shrugged.

"Sadie, Natalie!" Earl called out. Officer May and Sewer called their names again, too. Others down the line were calling out, listening for replies, but not hearing anything back. That sinking feeling in Earl's gut got worse by the minute. Fear was turning to panic, anxiety, and irritability. Who would take them? And if they were gone, *stolen*, what was happening to them right then?

He called their names, louder this time.

Nothing.

"It's not juvenile to consider the body's functions," Sewer practically mumbled, like he just had to talk, even though everyone wanted him to be quiet. "All I'm saying is that if you don't let out the gas, 'cause that's the rumbling going on, then you're going to have a category five mudslide on your hands."

Earl scoffed, but Officer May ignored him.

"Take a look around, Ma'am—you've got trees and scratchy bushes and a couple of rocks you can use to keep your butt off the ground, but no toilets."

"For the love of JESUS, kid, stay focused or go home!" Earl barked. He wasn't sure if he wanted to cry over the insanity he felt or beat the kid to a bloody pulp. "Sadie, Natalie!"

Coach intervened, calling out his daughters' names, like the others, but then he said, "What's going on over here, Stuart?"

"Nothin' Coach."

"Keep your eye on the ball," the old man said. "In this case, the ball is the task at hand, which is finding Earl's children."

Earl's cell phone vibrated in his back pocket. He pulled it out and saw a text from Gabby indicating she was home, but the girls were not there. His spirits plummeted further. He knew the drill: the longer they went missing, the worse their chances were of getting them back alive.

The search teams trudged through more forest, calling the girls' names and sweeping over the dark foliage with bright flashlights. By dawn, the remaining volunteers, most of whom he'd started with yesterday, were cold, bitten by insects, and so exhausted that most said they needed to pause the hunt to get a few hours of sleep.

Earl understood.

Many of these people had to tackle their normal days, but it would be tough with no sleep and an adrenaline dump from a hunt that had come up short. He was no different. But he couldn't give up the search for a single minute, nor could he focus on work or Gabby—who would call everyone she knew and more when the appropriate hour arose. Unfortunately, his wife was a near-manic wreck, and if she started drinking, there was no telling the version of her they would see.

Before he worked down in Mexico with a few other CIA officers infiltrating and disrupting the cartel networks, he worked in the sand as an operator, hunting down terrorists. He had been in plenty of scrapes, both in the Middle East and Mexico, and he'd lost friends and co-workers in both locales to cartel violence and war. He had also injured himself in Tijuana, Iraq, and Afghanistan; he had shrapnel in his left thigh from an exploded IED, no feeling in his three smallest fingers on his right hand from a bar fight, and more visible scars than stars on the flag. His head was one horror show after another after what he experienced. So why was he having such a hard time with this? But when he thought of Sadie and Natalie's faces, he knew. Sadie and Natalie were not men who signed up for the ballsiest, most dangerous jobs on the planet; they were two innocent girls—not even women yet.

When he returned home, Gabby met him on the front porch.

Her face hung heavy, her eyes bloodshot with bags under them, her arms crossed over a body weary with exhaustion.

Gabriella could be a mean drunk, but there was no doubt she loved their girls. "Nothin'?" she asked. Her eyes were as jumpy as anxious puppies.

"I'm scared," he finally admitted.

"Yeah, no kidding," she snapped. "We're all scared. But the girls have to be scared most, and we ain't doin' no good sittin' here jabbering on about it."

"Right now, yes, I agree," Earl said, bone tired and struggling to keep his eyes open. Gabby fixed him with a look he didn't like. "You drink anything today, Gabs?"

"No," she said, feigning insult.

"Usually, I have the patience to deal with you while you're on the sauce, but not now," he explained. "I wasn't trying to be rude; I was merely getting a lay of the land."

She made a face that said she understood. She didn't like it, but she understood. "I'll make calls in an hour," she promised. "You get some shut-eye, and we'll reconvene with the cops when you're up. Because if your buddy leaves us with Miss Fatty Pants and no answers, if he tries to call *that* a favor, I'm gonna crawl up his spine like a ladder and blow fire in his dog-ugly face until we get our girls back."

"First off, her name isn't Miss Fatty Pants, it's Officer May," he said. "There's respect due there since she was with us all night long, not feeling so hot on top of that."

Gabby waved a dismissive hand, then nodded her concession.

Earl swallowed hard and brushed off any other thoughts on the matter. Besides, his focus had turned elsewhere; he was hoping she'd be too busy making calls to get sloshed while he slept.

Shaking his head, he thought that the only thing worse than handling matters as "Mop Up" was dealing with Gabriella Gray in psycho mode.

six
officer teresa may

IT HAD STARTED with her lower back, then her hips, and then her feet, calves, and thighs. Everyone else was feeling it, too. Sewer's mom bowed out early on account of her feet and knees swelling, and one older gentleman checked out around three a.m., but everyone else vowed to press on. The teams took breaks, pooled their resources, and kept going because Earl and Gabby were determined. Teresa was determined, too. Everyone knew the first seventy-two hours were critical in a missing person's case; they had an early start and had to make the most of it.

"My shit feels *beat up*," Sewer complained, shuffling beside her.

He had remained faithfully at her side all night, unwilling to throw in the towel. She gained enough respect for him to call him Stuart after all this. Maybe. But not yet.

Now that parts of her legs and butt had gone numb, it seemed her upper body chose to carry the torch of pain. The heat and poking needles ran the length of her back, settling into her shoulders and trapezius muscles. Teresa wasn't a complainer, though, not while she wore the badge and carried her gun. Still, the way her mind went wild with every possible scenario for finding a body or two filled her head with cotton at times and nightmares at other times. Was this an effective strategy for planning to encounter dead children? Or was she a rookie in a tough spot? Probably a bit of both, but time would tell.

The acid indigestion that resulted from wolfing down her sandwich had died down a bit, but her lower colon felt lousy, and her gut had since filled and refilled itself with gas. She burped but was too tired to excuse herself. Sewer grunted next to her. Teresa didn't care.

One foot in front of the other, she told herself.

So, she moved forward, continued scanning the ground, checking in larger bushes, and walking around outcroppings and fallen trees—anywhere one might leave a body. She also continued to call out the girls' names when her throat wasn't killing her, albeit with less enthusiasm than before, and she checked left and right to see if anyone had found anything of interest. The Chain Saw sandwich had officially put her stomach into maximum distress, her belly rumbling so loudly sometimes that she cleared her throat or walked heavier to cover her sounds. Twice, she had reassured Sewer she wasn't squeezing cheese on the job. Both times she lied.

Finally, after daybreak, a few holdouts threw in the towel, but not Teresa. She told herself she and Earl would be the last to leave, so no one could say she'd quit on the girls. Most everyone left, including Earl, who thanked her before leaving.

She made the slow trek up the road, heading to her cruiser, where she had left it parked on Rattlesnake Road. Her feet were numb, her uniform dirty, and her hair hung in a messy ponytail. She studied every house she passed, searching for people to talk with or security systems that might have captured what human eyes missed.

A Cape Cod-style house perched high above Oak Ridge Drive, across from Oak Meadows, looked promising. Teresa spotted a small white rectangle mounted over the garage door—a surveillance camera if she was lucky. She headed in for a closer look, just to be sure. Within a few minutes, Teresa had climbed to the top of the steep concrete driveway and confirmed the camera's existence. She turned and looked down onto the roads and bus stop below. The camera had the perfect view for getting answers. She prayed the owners had recorded and stored the scene yesterday and that the department could access whatever video footage was available without the need for a warrant. After taking notes, Teresa thought of knocking on the door, but she checked the time, realized it was still too early, and left the scene.

She made a note to pull the county records and see if Chief Davenport would call the owner, maybe pave the way for her to visit after she had a hot shower, a few hours' shuteye, and a fresh uniform. As it was, she smelled woodsy, but with the locker room stench of body odor.

Teresa was only fifty yards from her cruiser when a horrible churning sensation seized her stomach. She stopped, gulped, and looked up at the sky with a pained expression on her face. Had too much gas backed up into her belly? Because it was now pushing into her lungs.

"My God," she mumbled, remembering the last time this happened.

She resumed her trek but with a fresh hitch in her walk. She drew her hand to her belly and scanned the area for a place to squat if she was having an emergency, which she was. Then, she felt a "popped-bubble" sensation, a moment's relief, and a sudden return to the churning. She began to sweat. Licking her lips, she pushed loose strands of hair from her face and wiped the perspiration from her forehead. When she finally reached her cruiser, Teresa climbed in, sighed deeply, and called Avery at dispatch.

"Thought you went home," he said.

"I'm coming in now."

"Roger that."

Everyone had gone home; it was just her, and the silence around her was pressing. But then came the rumbling gut again, the squeezing pain, and a low, escaping moan.

The pain was too much, so she got out of her car because things were moving like a washer on a spin cycle. The second she was outside, the back pressure released, and she unleashed the mother of all farts. It was a blue-ribbon ripper, starting slow and barky but picking up speed with the promise of becoming something special. When it struck a high point, she quietly thanked Jesus for the relief and promptly snapped it off.

"I knew you been farting all night," the voice behind her said.

Startled, she spun around and saw Sewer Jones sitting on his bicycle like a scrub. How the hell did he sneak up on her like that? Ugh, she needed better situational awareness! Panicking, she searched for one of a thousand things to say, but what do you say in a situation like hers? Not a damn thing, that's what.

"And they call *me* Sewer," he mumbled.

"Mind your own business," she snapped, her face beet red.

"I could get you some toilet paper since it sounds like you need it, Officer Cabbage Pants. Or I could not worry about it and *mind my business* elsewhere."

"Why are you here anyway?" she asked, annoyed that she had worked hard all night not to have an embarrassing outburst only to have this hamflower ride right into its breeze.

He cleared his throat and said, "I wanted to say I shoulda been more respectful of you earlier on accounta you being a cop, but that was just cover for what I really wanted to say."

"And what's that?" she asked, swallowing hard.

He looked at her as if getting up his courage, then said, "I was thinking you were hot for 5-0. But then you went and cooked up that Kentucky Mudslide, and now I'm thinking the single life is for me."

The audacity of this twerp!

"Your balls haven't even dropped, and you're quitting the dating pool already?" she asked with laughter. "If you want a girlfriend, you have to know that women are just as gross as men, so while you're picking your nose and scratching your ass tonight, and wondering if God has true love in store for a knucklehead like you, just know He probably does, but it'll come at a price."

"So, it seems," he said, holding his nose for effect. Then, with a dismissive chuckle, he turned his bike around and began pedaling down Rattlesnake Drive, back to his diabetic momma with her busted knees and two collapsed feet.

"Little turd," she spat. She opened the cruiser door, heard the radio, and checked in.

"What's your 20?" Avery asked.

"Still at Rattlesnake Drive," she replied. "Haven't left yet due to an uncomfortable encounter with Sewer Jones."

She released the mic button and waited for a reply. None came. She didn't want to give Avery the details, not on a recorded line.

Avery opened the mic to clear his throat, then closed the line again. Had this just become a game of waiting him out? What the hell did he want her to say? Finally, he opened the line and said, "I thought you were 10-24."

"Yeah, I thought I was finished, too."

The silence stretched.

"What was uncomfortable about an encounter with Sewer?" Avery finally asked.

"I'm heading in, over."

"How'd that sandwich hit you this time?" Avery pressed as if struggling to hold back the laughter.

"It's been hitting me like a 10-31 if you want the truth." *A crime in progress.*

"That bad?" he asked.

"It almost became a 10-52," she grinned. *A call for an ambulance.*

Avery snorted out a laugh. "I can have one on standby if you need it. What's your 101?"

"Are you practicing your 10 codes or something?" she asked.

"What's your 101?" he repeated.

"My status, *Avery*, is I'm tired, this Chain Saw sandwich has been an angry badger running loose in my gut all night, and now I've got to worry about a kid called 'Sewer' talking crap about me to everyone in town. No pun intended."

"Really," he said. "What for?"

"Let me put it to you this way: if that obnoxious nitwit runs his mouth about what just happened to me, I won't have any date nights anytime soon, not with the local guys anyway."

Avery quietly said, "Look on the bright side..."

"Oh, there's a bright side?"

Deadpan, with perfect delivery, Avery said, "Most guys wouldn't have you anyway, but you didn't hear that from me."

Her mouth fell open. Then, with fire in her eyes, she leaned into the radio and growled, "That was me who told you that, *moron!*"

seven
officer teresa may

TERESA CHECKED into the precinct before heading home to catch the chief fresh. Everyone who saw her tried pulling her aside to get the 411 on the hunt for the girls, but all she could do was shake her head, tell them she hadn't slept yet, and make a beeline for Chief Davenport's office.

Someone she snubbed said, "Rude," to which she replied, "Yes, but not on purpose."

The truth was that everything hurt; she could hardly walk, and she felt muscle, fat, and loose skin all hanging off her bones like oversized clothes. Worse, her hair and hands were dirty, and she reeked of body odor, reminding her of her younger brother when he was going through puberty. Back then, he used to work out with weights for hours, then grab her and shove her face into his armpits while telling her, "That's what a *man* smells like!"

She managed to push him away and say, "If that's how all men smell, I'm going to be a lesbian when I grow up!"

"Too late!" he said, snubbing her.

She did not grow up to be a lesbian, but she had managed to avoid most men. Instead of dating, she went to the police academy, bought a dog for company, and made a few close friends. For now, that was enough.

"It seems this case is going to keep you busy," Chief Davenport said when he saw her. He waved her in, getting a good look at her. "Best you make some progress before folks bring up the other girls again."

"The other girls, Chief?"

He rolled his eyes and said, "Oh, c'mon, you know."

She frowned and said, "Coach is already talking about it. Same with Earl. I tried to put the kibosh on it, but it's already a topic."

"But did they say it?" he asked.

She shook her head because neither man said the words *serial killer*. "Would they be wrong if they did?" Teresa asked.

"No, Officer May," Chief Davenport replied in a curt tone. "I don't think they would be wrong."

"If we were dealing with a serial, wouldn't we have a workable MO? I mean, can we match any of this to previous patterns?"

"You tell me," Davenport said, pinching his features like he hated the entire discussion.

"I can't say for sure, so I suggest we treat it as a case of missing persons. If that changes, maybe we'll have a different conversation then."

"Don't be so damn naïve," he grumbled. "You know this is just like the others."

"Is there anything wrong with having optimism, Chief Davenport?"

He breathed deeply through his nose, narrowed his unblinking eyes, then breathed audibly and said, "Optimism is something others get to have. But not you. You know how bad people can be, Officer May."

"Missing girls don't always equal dead girls," she said.

"That'll be the case with my friend's girls."

She stared at him long enough to show her grit but not so long that it came off as a challenge to his authority. For the last twelve hours, she had tried to force those two terrible words from her head over and over again, if anything, to maintain hope that the girls were still alive.

"We're not dealing with a serial killer," she finally said.

Chief Davenport said, "I'm done with this conversation, Officer May."

"Before I leave," she said, sliding a slip of paper across his desk, "I saw a camera mounted over a garage, facing the bus stop, and I'm thinking you or the L.T. can call the homeowner and get us access to the recording."

"If they recorded it, we should be able to get it without a warrant," he said. "We only need to ask kindly or be convincing if that doesn't work."

Teresa nodded, praying the homeowner's system was active.

"I'll text you the number, and you can ask them on my behalf," Chief Davenport said. "If they say no, I'll get on the phone with them."

"Time is of the essence," she said.

"I know that."

She didn't let the chief's gruff nature intimidate her. "You or the L.T. could call while I'm recharging my batteries."

"Or we could empower you, and maybe you sleep a little less," he said.

She was only an officer if she acted like one, and, in so many words, he told her to act like one. If she thought about it, if the chief was truly in her corner, then how she handled this case could very well determine the trajectory of her career in law enforcement at Grass Valley PD.

The chief suddenly smiled and said, "Thanks for working overtime. I'll be sure to adjust the hourly wage."

"Yeah, sure," Teresa said. "Thanks."

"Get some sleep, a shower, and something to eat," he said, sounding congenial again. "We're going to see this thing through."

"Like we saw the other missing girls' cases through?" she

asked flippantly. The second she caught his ire she regretted making the statement. "I'm sorry, I'm just tired."

"You know we're never going to find the other girls, not without a new case, similar MOs, and a cold case staff, which you know doesn't exist."

"What about the Feds?"

"Me and the suits don't play well together. They're a bunch of hoity-toity cockbags who'll end up tearing this station apart long before they solve any real cases. We would need something catastrophic to bring them in, mark my words."

"Let's see what happens with Earl," she said. "The man seems ready to set the entire world on fire."

"Didn't you hear me say 'we're done'?"

"Yes, Sir, I did."

"Then why are you still standing here?"

"If staffing ever changes for the better, I can jump on the cold cases, see if anything's changed."

He nodded and said, "After we find the girls, maybe. For now, as long as we can get the community involved, we'll have free labor and many eyes. But the second they give up hope, they'll turn away or turn on us. You know that, right?"

She nodded and said, "I do."

"Go home and shower, Teresa—you stink."

"Yes, Sir."

The chief nodded and looked back at his computer, typing something, which was an apparent dismissal. Teresa nodded and left quietly.

On the way out of the precinct, the people who tried stopping her earlier glanced up, hoping for details, but she avoided eye contact. Instead, she went straight home and found that her dog, Homer—a snorty little pug—had pooped in the house and eaten one of the house plants. Worse than that, he ripped off one of the couch cushions and started chewing on it.

"The hell, Homer?" Teresa said when she walked inside her

apartment. How could she blame the little guy when she left him alone for *way too long?*

The pug was sitting on the couch where he had ripped off the cushion as if it was the best place ever. Teresa admonished him with her eyes, even though it was no fault of the dog, and took a calming breath. Worse things than half-eaten cushions had plagued the day.

Homer looked down, tried to pretend Teresa wasn't there, then hopped off the couch. He trotted like a prince over to his empty bowl and looked down at it.

"It's not gonna fill itself up just because you're looking at it," she said, walking to the mutt. She bent and scratched Homer behind his ears and under his belly. "Not your fault, little guy. This one's on me."

She gave Homer extra kibble, which he lapped up in seconds. When finished, he looked up at Teresa with those big, hypnotic eyes but remained over the bowl.

"For real?" she asked. The dog let out a sharp bark. "Keep eating like a pig, and you're gonna turn into one someday."

Within a few minutes, she put her cushion back on the couch, plopped onto it without taking off anything but her shoes and belt, and fell asleep. Homer jumped on top of the sofa, walked over the top of her, then wedged his warm little body into the space between her and the couch's back cushions. Soon, he was asleep and snoring in her ear. It would have been cute had Teresa not needed the sleep. The snorty, trumpeting noise faded as she drifted off into a dark, dreamless slumber, one she had longed for since midnight last night. But that didn't last long. The first call woke her right away. Two pushes sent the call to voicemail and she put the phone to vibrate mode. The phone began vibrating before she could fall asleep. Now, it rattled across the coffee table, knocking around the glass. Homer barked in her ear.

"No, Homer," she said while silencing the phone.

The pug lay his head back down and snorted. When the

phone vibrated a third time, she realized she was not getting any sleep and that it was best to get up and push through the day.

When she checked the call logs, she found they had come from two women at the precinct, collectively known as the gossip squad. There was no way she was taking those calls. Instead, she dialed her neighbor's phone number, a guy she met last year. They shared recipes, eggs, milk occasionally, and movie reviews.

"Teresa," he said, picking up.

"I need you to watch my dog if you can."

"Of course," he replied. He worked from home but was also a gamer nerd, which meant he was always home.

"How soon can you come and get him?"

"If I do this for you, I want something in return."

She felt her blood starting to warm. He had never asked for anything in return, but maybe things were changing. "Yes?" she asked, tempering her response.

"I want you to take me out on a date," he said confidently. "You know I'm not social and don't get out enough."

"For a reason, I'm sure."

"You're the only human I know and like in real life, and I want someone to do something special for me, so that's my price."

She ran a hand through her hair, looked around the small apartment to keep from telling him to pound sand, and said, "All right, on one condition."

"Name it," he said, perking up.

"I pay."

"Which means you don't owe me sex for the free meal?"

"That's right," she grinned.

"Less fun than I thought, but—"

"I'm still a virgin and expect to stay that way," she said with a liar's grin.

"I'm a virgin, too," he said, "four times over. But don't worry about me. I'm all about goodwill, and this will earn me some."

"It earns you a night on the town with me and my amazing

company," she yawned. "If you want anything else, hire a hooker."

"Fair enough," he said. "Bring the snorter over."

"See you in five."

She sat up, rubbed her eyes, and looked at Homer.

"You're going next door," she said. He whined. "No back talk. You destroyed the place while I was gone, and though that is partially my fault, you need to take some responsibility for your actions, too."

He barked.

The vibrating phone interrupted her again. She wanted to flush the damn thing down the toilet or drop it into the sink disposal. Instead, she picked it up and said, "Yeah."

"You asleep?" Chief Davenport asked.

"Yes, Sir, soundly."

"Good," he said. "I got the phone number to the house with the surveillance camera, but no one's answering my calls, so when you get up, head over there and see if they'll come to the door."

"Who are they, Sir?"

"Older couple, maybe a widow. I don't have time to pull records, but you have time to ask for yourself, in the flesh, so to speak. L.T.'s texting you the details."

"Okay."

"So?" he asked.

Have I missed something?

"Yeah?"

"This is your first lead, Officer May."

"Oh, okay," she said, rubbing her face. If she smelled bad before, it had somehow gotten worse.

"More good news," the chief continued. "I should be getting a K-9 unit out here later this afternoon, on loan from Nevada County."

She perked up—another solid development.

"Okay, then. Let me shower, grab a coffee, and return to the scene."

"You're front and center until we have a body."

"Or two," she added.

"Let's hope we find them alive and not... *you know*," he said. "The department can't go through that again."

"Neither can the parents," Teresa added.

"Of course."

Clues leading to girls missing from years prior had seemed promising to the detectives assigned to the case, but everything dried up. It was the same with every missing girl. Fortunately, Teresa wasn't at the precinct then, but everyone knew the particulars. It was the town's open secret. If Chief Davenport could just keep things quiet, and not call it what it was—a serial killer—then the good folks of Grass Valley could continue mourning the girls without freaking out every minute of the day. But, if they hit a wall during this newest investigation, Teresa would head to their cold case files on her own time and look for similarities, maybe even craft a workable MO.

And if we get a body or bodies? That question had been banging around in her head since the search began.

If she found one or both of the girls, she could hand the case over to seasoned detectives and go back to issuing tickets, making community stops, and speaking to school kids about making smart decisions and understanding the rule of law.

Teresa stood and stretched, feeling every uneven mile of terrain she'd walked last night in her feet, ankles, and knees. Then, the discomfort hit her lower back with a pinch that stopped her cold. Glancing down, she scowled at a dog turd lying on the carpet, along the edge of the couch.

"You still there?" Chief Davenport asked. She thought he hung up—he hadn't.

Clearing her throat, she said, "I'm gonna need a breakfast burrito on the way in if you've got someone running for chow. That'll get me knocking on doors far sooner."

"You sure you're okay with a burrito after what The Chain Saw did to you?"

Mortified, she gasped. Shame burned brightly on her cheeks, and she didn't want to say it, but she was still dealing with the aftereffects of the sandwich.

"Don't worry, Officer," the chief said with a glint of humor, "I'll have one of the guys grab a mild one for you. Text me your order and get to that house, Code 3, if you have to."

"Yes, Sir," she said.

If this is how the day is going to start, she thought with a frown, *ten bucks and an A-1 burger say it'll all go to hell before noon.*

eight
sadie gray

I DIDN'T KNOW if it was day or night, but the second I woke up to the sounds of many feet walking all over the floorboards above me, I knew it wasn't fully dark yet. I glanced over to see about Natalie, but our own darkness held us captive and blinded us. If I stared into it long enough, would it be the same as looking into deep space?

Maybe.

The door at the top of the wooden stairs opened, the overhead bulb illuminated, and heavy feet tromped down every wooden step, the full weight of the monster descending upon us. I wanted to look over at Natalie, but I dared not try. I did, however, discreetly turn my head to keep an eye on the enemy.

When I saw the brute's face and body, the horror returned, and I wanted to run so badly I damn near came out of my skin. He carried a small plate of biscuits, two total. He gave one to Natalie and one to me. He set both biscuits within reach.

"You need your energy for dying," he said, smiling as he spoke to us in a kind, almost paternal voice. "The fighting will take a lot out of you, but ultimately, it will be good for the customers."

"This is an actual business?" I asked, flabbergasted.

He nodded and said, "In the long run, it doesn't matter what we want most in life; we only need to monetize and sell it. I learned that online."

"You're the first serial killer I know of to try making a business out of it," Sadie grumbled. A poor sleep and endless nightmares left her feeling like a rag doll.

He tapped his temple with a meaty finger and said, "Capitalism isn't just for the select few, young lady. The best businessmen say you should embrace your hobby, find your customers, and build your base. And do you know what?"

"You found your base," I said.

He nodded and said, "Eat them biscuits, Sugar. They were fresh a few days ago, so time is of the essence." He laughed as he said that, and then he went back upstairs. Fortunately, he left the light on, which allowed me to lift my head and see Natalie.

She was looking back at me, then at the biscuit, and then at the video camera. Beyond that, I saw a mound of stuffed animals, an old dresser with colorful stickers on the drawer faces, and some jewelry resembling a trophy pile of plastic costume jewelry.

That was when I realized Natalie wasn't looking at the stuffed animals or creepy décor with me; she was studying the dried blood stains on the walls and floors. And then she was yanking like a lunatic on her restraints. Finally, she gave up the fight and toppled over on her side, crying helplessly.

The door at the top of the stairs opened once more, followed by a fresh set of footsteps descending the stairs. These feet hit each step, lighter and less confident than the man before. A small girl suddenly appeared, dressed for school. She saw us but wasn't surprised.

"Who are you?" I asked.

"The daughter."

She had to be Natalie's age.

"Can you get us out of these?" Natalie turned and asked, shaking her hands to display the ropes.

"He'll take you out when he's done with you."

Sadie could not believe a girl this age was acting so numb or speaking so candidly about torture and abuse.

"Your daddy," I heard myself say in a voice shaking with outrage, "you realize he hurts people, right? That he's going to hurt us."

The girl smiled and nodded, almost as if proud. She looked like one of the twins from *The Shining*.

"Do you want us to get hurt?" Natalie asked.

The girl picked up a stuffed teddy bear and said, "I like the sounds of screaming. I can't scream or even cry—he won't let us. So, when the ones like you scream, it makes me smile."

"He's your father, right?" Natalie asked. The girl nodded. "Where's your mother?"

"Dead." A smile.

"How'd she die?" I asked.

"Hammer."

With that, she turned and headed back upstairs, snapped off the light, and crossed the floor overhead.

"Did you know she lived here?" I asked my sister. Natalie didn't speak. Was she in shock?

"I need to pee, Sadie," she finally said. "I can't hold it any longer."

"Just go, then."

"I'm so scared," Natalie said, her voice shaking.

I grabbed the ropes that bound me to the bed and started tugging at them fiercely at first, then supercharged with rage, and then less manic as the rest of my energy bled out. *Should I eat the biscuit and get that energy?* Maybe I had to. All I knew was that I couldn't die, not while Natalie was still alive. Nothing bad could happen to my sister—nothing!

I sniffed the biscuit, and it smelled old and stale. Part of me wanted to devour it, but what if he laced it with something poisonous? My stomach felt so hollow. Slowly shaking my head, I decided not to eat it until I was really, *really* hungry.

As I lay there, terrified to die without trying harder to live, I couldn't help thinking of all those times Natalie and I hid under the blankets, listening to our parents fighting. Too often, our mom smelled like alcohol, and our dad got upset and broke stuff, yelling for her to stop drinking. But she loved to drink, and she said *stuff* when she was drunk, not all of it nice like a good mom should tell her kids. If we survived that nightmare, we could survive this one, couldn't we?

I felt the start of something new and powerful growing inside me, a renewed strength in my bones. Dad would call this "determination." We had to get out of this monster's house, graduate from high school, and start our own lives. Then we'd have to leave this crap town and never come home again—not until we were grown women who could stand up for ourselves and leave any time we wanted if things got too bad.

But the creep who took us was worse than our parents. And his weird daughter scared me almost as much as her father. They both shocked and angered me so much that I didn't realize I was screaming until the stomping on the floorboards overhead startled me into silence.

"Hey!" the man's voice upstairs boomed. "You keep making all that noise, and I'm gonna come down there and staple your lips shut."

I stopped moving long enough to realize my eyes were leaking and I might be losing my mind. I turned on my side and caught sight of my sister. She lay there in a puddle of urine, quietly crying to herself, unable or unwilling to meet my eyes.

nine
earl "mop up" gray

EARL SLEPT on the couch because Gabby had become a zombie and wouldn't let him console her. He wasn't sure if her not drinking was just as bad as her being drunk. It was a coin toss at that point. In the end, being around her didn't seem like an option. Despite the sun being up, he drifted off to sleep for a few hours. He woke himself and went to check on Gabby; she was sound asleep.

Instead of mulling about the house or making calls, he dressed, threw on a hat, and grabbed his keys and wallet. He kissed Gabby on the cheek before leaving, then went to the truck. The old Dodge started right away. He spotted his folding knife sitting on the seat and tucked it into his pocket, then he put the rig in gear and headed out to resume the search.

He had been knocking on doors and talking to folks along Oak Meadows Drive when he saw Officer May walking up the steep driveway of a Cape Cod-style house perched on a small hilltop. He didn't know the owners personally and hadn't seen them out or around their house, even though he passed the home a hundred times or more.

He jogged up the street, trudged up the concrete driveway, and met Officer May on the front porch. She didn't look so happy to see him. Either that or last night's search party had worn her out completely.

"That an active surveillance camera I saw?" he asked, pointing to a small unit mounted above the garage door.

She nodded and knocked on the door.

"Whatcha doing out here so early, Officer?" he asked, wishing she were more conversational and less... quiet.

"Not giving up early," she finally said.

"This your first stop?"

Instead of answering with her words, she nodded and motioned to the camera. "Saw it earlier this morning."

"Did someone try calling first?"

"Chief did earlier," she replied, knocking harder this time. "No one answered, so I thought I'd come here and try in person."

Earl turned and looked out onto the road. The house had a perfect view of the street near the bus stop, which could not just confirm the girls getting off the bus but could also provide clues as to what happened after that. With the homes primarily situated on three- to five-acre parcels, most of them set back into their property, the surveillance camera in question was their best chance at moving the search forward.

When no one answered the door, Earl asked, "What now?"

"I'll head around back, see if I can see inside," she said, brushing past him. "You wait here."

She walked around the back; he followed her. She glanced over her shoulder, saw him, and stopped, then turned to face him. Frowning, she said, "I'd appreciate it if you would let me do my job, Mr. Gray."

"While you're doing your job as an officer, I'll be doing mine as a parent."

"Suit yourself," she said. "But, for the record, I told you not to come, and you were defiant."

"I prefer to think of it as insistent."

"Same thing in the court's eyes," she continued. "You're violating a direct order from law enforcement."

"Sounds about right."

She stopped and faced him again, her eyes hardened like a cop's in trying situations. "I was willing to overlook your bad reputation, Mr. Gray, but you're earning it right now. You know that, don't you?"

He frowned. "We're wasting time, Teresa."

When she didn't budge, he walked around her, but she caught up to him and walked around him, retaking the lead. It was a bit childish, but she didn't mention his defiance or bad reputation this time.

They saw another camera past the slider, ignored it, and peeked through the windows and slider in the back of the house.

"Looks empty," Earl said.

"Yeah."

They peered through the dusty sliding glass door, looked around the darkened kitchen, and absorbed even the smallest details, hoping for a story on the homeowners' whereabouts. Finally, Earl slapped his palm hard on the glass, loud enough that someone would have heard it, but no one did.

"You working today?" she finally asked.

"Can't afford not to, but I'm gonna try to get the day off," he lied. "I need to go in for that. Boss says no one calls in sick, but if you show up and you're sick, he'll send you home."

"Good policy," she said with a nod. "Weeds out the slackers."

"You only coming here, or…?"

"I'm going to canvas the entire neighborhood until someone tells me something," she said. "Chief has a K-9 unit coming later today. He's trying to get a chopper, too."

"Skip came through, then," he said.

She eyed him briefly, then asked, "How do you and the chief know each other?"

"Army buddies," he answered. "We saw some things, did some things, and forged a bond in the suck, as the Marines say. Even if you don't much like each other—and we're not besties by any stretch—the sand has a way of gluing guys like us together."

Officer May nodded. "I respect that."

"I'll find you after I get clearance from work." He pulled out his phone and said, "What's your number?"

"I'm not giving you my private number."

"Just for texting," he said, staring at his phone and not at her. "C'mon, quit messing around." Reluctantly, she shook her head, pulled out her phone, and gave him the number. He sent her a text and then said, "If you get any decent footage," he motioned to the other camera, "I want to know right away."

"I'll text you as soon as I have something to let you in on."

"Thanks," he said.

Officer May seemed relieved that he was leaving, but her relief was the last thing she'd feel if she knew what he was contemplating. Then again, Earl had no idea about the nightmare he was about to crawl into, this time head-first.

ten
sadie gray

THE CREEP plodded downstairs with a different look in his eye this time. He glared at us both and said, "I got all the pictures I needed, and now it's time to take the video." As he licked his lips, his cold eyes became hungry eyes, which made me want to vomit.

He turned his attention to Natalie, where she lay on the floor. Standing over the top of her, looking down, he said, "You pissed yourself?"

Natalie refused to answer. He bent low, swiped his finger through the liquid, then stood tall and suckled on his finger. "Yep, urine."

Looking pleased, he grabbed a camera and photographed it.

"There's an innocence to dying, don't you think?" he asked, looking at me when he spoke. He continued talking before I even had a chance to answer. "We all do it differently and only get to do it once. We hope there's no pain because we can't still believe in God if He lets us suffer the way I'm going to make you two suffer."

If I needed confirmation that he was going to kill us, I just got it. Worse, he's going to do it *right now*.

He set the camera on a nearby stand and said, "When they find your bodies, *if* they ever find them, your parents will question everything they know and believe." His eyes glistened with happiness. "They will never be the same, because parents with dead kids don't survive that sort of thing intact. So, really, in taking your two lives, I'm taking four. Do you know how exciting that is?"

My outrage now overshadowed my fear. "You can't even say God's name, you filthy freak."

With deeply amused eyes, he said, "Look at you, fourteen and built like a boy. You'll pass for younger for a few of my customers, but your sister here—she's not even ten years old, which is perfect for my audience. Once we undress her, it will be about choosing how she goes, you know? Hammer, shovel, sledgehammer—that's a good one—chainsaw?"

"They're going to find you, and when they do—"

"Who's going to find me?" he boomed, his voice so explosive that Natalie and I jumped at once.

"Just let us go, please," I heard myself say.

He smiled again, trying to disarm me with a warm expression; it wouldn't work. Or maybe he was trying to get me to give up or cooperate—two things I'd never do.

"I once took a girl's body apart with a skill saw," he said as if it was nothing. "Took a while, and it was super messy, but I got twenty-five large for the video. The guy was a camp counselor. I mean, I know there are some real psychos out there, but I had no idea guys like that were flush with cash. Then again, you know what they say: 'Where there's a will, there's a way.' I can tell you one thing—that man found a way."

It was all I could do to hold my stomach down.

The creep returned his gaze to Natalie. "Stand up, or I'll kill you where you lie, child." Natalie didn't move; I started to cry, which angered me. "If you stand, I'll make it quick and painless, like with the sledgehammer. But if you act like a dead fish, I'll stuff your hands into a blender, and then your feet. And then I'll feed each limb into the blender until you're just an armless, legless abomination, bleeding to death all over the floor."

I wanted to tell Natalie to stand up and get it over quickly, but how could I do that?

The creep considered his words and the situation as if mulling it over and finally said, "I bet I could get at least twenty grand for a blender death. So, go ahead and lay there, you stupid, *stupid* child."

Natalie shifted, pulled her arms under her, and pushed herself to her feet. She was shaking so badly and quietly crying, but she also stood before this animal and faced him. I could never do that. I wasn't that brave. That was when I heard a commotion upstairs, followed by someone pounding on a door.

"Congratulations, young lady," the creep said to Natalie, "you get the sledgehammer." Then he looked at me with a frown. "But your sister gets the blender."

Fresh horror coursed through my veins.

The basement door flew open, and from the top of the stairs, a boy said, "Dad, someone's at the door!"

With that, the creep headed upstairs and snapped off the overhead light, leaving Natalie and me alone in the dark, fearing for our deaths.

I tracked him by the sounds his feet made on the floorboards. When I heard him stop, I listened even closer. When I heard voices, I turned to Natalie and said, "Start screaming as loud as you can."

Each of us took the deepest breaths we've ever taken in our lives, and then we let out the mother of all screams, both of us giving it all we had despite our raw throats.

eleven
officer teresa may

TERESA WALKED up the long dirt driveway, checking for guard dogs or armed homeowners. Her stomach growled, but she ignored it. Unfortunately, her stomach still bothered her, but not because she was hungry.

She headed to the front door, knowing she couldn't eat whatever burrito the guys from the station had bought her. The coffee she drank too quickly had mixed with last night's sandwich and was now hitting her harder than she thought.

The second she raised a fist to knock on the door, her stomach made a forceful grumble, one wet enough and meaty enough to let her know that The Chain Saw hadn't exited yet, but it was about to.

A sheen of perspiration mapped her brow, and sweat beaded along her hairline, rolling slowly down her forehead. She wiped them away, suddenly feeling faint. Then, she suffered a stabbing pain under her ribs, one ferocious enough for her to reconsider the very notion of doing today's duties. And why did she still feel so damn full?

Her phone buzzed in her pocket. She pulled it out, thinking she wasn't ready to talk to Earl, not with last night's mistake working to become this morning's shame. But it wasn't a call; the vibration was a text message. Teresa wiped her head again, then her eyes, and then she read the text from the precinct. She huffed out loud. The text said a breakfast burrito awaited her when she got to the station. Her stomach rolled, and she swallowed so hard she didn't think she would last two minutes without a bathroom. And the idea of a burrito? No. Hell no!

Her stomach was now a clenched fist inside her, moving hard and causing incredible discomfort. It let out a low growl that left her hunched over and on the verge of tears. Whatever was going on wouldn't be alleviated by a simple, space-making fart.

In the distance, farther down the property, a young blonde girl in a dress carrying a teddy bear wandered into what looked like remnants of an old concrete building perched along the creek. Was that a failed water wheel? Farther to the right, on the other side of the creek, she spotted Earl Gray's house. She didn't realize she had gone so far but knew one thing: she needed a bathroom quickly.

Her stomach shifted and sank as she knocked on the front door. No one answered right away, and she couldn't hold it much longer; her shins were cramping, and she was sweating profusely now. She knocked, much louder this time.

Oh, dear God, it's coming.

Her face felt cold and clammy, and she just knew that whoever lived here would have to let her use the can, or she was going to crap herself.

She knocked again, pounding this time, and was surprised when the door opened to reveal a familiar face.

"Oh, thank God, Coach," she said. "I didn't know you lived here."

He smiled and said, "Did you find the girls yet?"

The elevator in her stomach was about to hit the ground floor, and she was desperate.

"You okay, Officer?"

A violent sloshing hit the bottom of her gut, causing her to buckle and swear off The Chain Saw sandwich forever. And that was when she heard screaming coming from inside the house—

the faint sounds of girls' voices asking for help from below the floorboards.

The second that happened, Coach's eyes flashed, as did hers, and she backed up so fast that her bowels let go while she was trying to draw her weapon. Her abdominal pains and the horrible untimely accident gave Coach Tilly the advantage. He had a gun, too, which Teresa hadn't realized, and he moved quickly for an older guy.

He fired the first shot before she could get her first round off. The bullet punched her in the side of the face so hard it knocked her backward. He shot her again, this time in the chest, and that was the one that did it.

Wobbling on shaky legs, with her mind moving both slowly and lightning-fast, she wanted to return fire, but the gun slid from her hand and fell into the dirt.

Coach merely stared at her.

Her leg finally gave out; she collapsed to a knee. Half the world had faded to black, and she didn't have the balance or strength to stand, so she toppled sideways into the dirt, bleeding badly, her pants still filling with crap.

twelve
earl "mop up" gray

EARL HAD LIED to Officer May when he said he had to check in with the job. Not only did he lie, but he also didn't feel bad about it. The second he watched her leave the house and head up the road, he texted his buddy at the Agency—a former case agent turned cyber security expert.

"Oh, boy," he said. That was how he answered the call.

Earl skipped the pleasantries and said, "I need to access a Eufy home security system."

"You want it shut down, or do you need the data?"

"Data."

"Okay, hang on."

A few minutes later, he said, "Alexa can connect the system, and it's password-protected with decent encryption. Give me a minute or two more."

"Roger that," Earl said.

His friend was back on the line shortly. "It was hard to figure out, but I got it. You need to know, though, that you took up two minutes I'll never get back."

"Meaning?"

"You owe me, Earl."

"Someone took my girls," Earl said.

A slight pause. "Never mind, then. This one's on the house.

The Blinding Light

I'm sending you a link now. Once you're inside the interface, you'll have fifteen minutes of access. Text me when you finish, and I'll close the link and sweep up behind you."

"Roger that," he said.

The link came through after they ended the call. Earl pressed it, waited a moment, and watched the screen change as he gained access to the dashboard. If his friend said it took him two minutes to hack the app, and he was one of the best hackers Earl knew, the system was rock solid.

Once he was in, the user interface was easy to navigate, especially the playback dates and times. He returned to the time when his girls' bus appeared to drop them off. A moment later, he watched them exit the bus and walk down the street. The sight of Sadie and Natalie caused him to well up. A van entered the camera's relatively wide field of view, stopping at the edge of the screen. A familiar-looking man got out.

Earl's stomach dropped. "No way," he muttered.

When the girls approached him, Coach Tilly started talking and pointed to a nearby field. When Sadie glanced into the field, the coach grabbed Natalie and slammed her head into the side of the van. Sadie ran, and he ran after her.

At that moment, Earl Gray transformed into Mop Up, and everything was about to get real. He knew that van, that face, and what he was about to do. The man lived next door; he'd helped spearhead last night's search! Could the girls have been locked up at his house the whole time?

He jumped into his truck, threw it into gear, and cranked the wheel, fishtailing the back end in a dusty fit. The tires barked when they first encountered the asphalt, and the old truck jolted forward. He took the familiar roads like he was driving an Audi rather than an old Dodge pickup because every second mattered.

The minute he arrived at Coach Tilly's house, he saw Officer May's cruiser parked along the road; he spotted her at the front door, maybe fifty yards away. He killed the engine with a feral growl, ready to go in with her and get the girls. But then he heard the gunshot and watched Teresa's head snap back. As if the scene unfolded in slow motion, Earl then watched Teresa stagger backward, stumbling. She tried to lift her gun. A second shot rang out, the bullet striking the female officer's chest. Earl let out a breath. The senseless killing doubled his heartbeat and pumped his bloodstream full of adrenaline.

He leaned over, opened the glovebox, and grabbed his old man's revolver—a Taylor's & Co. Cattleman .45 single-action revolver. It was a true wrist-breaker and louder than hell, but comfortable in his hand. He checked the cylinder, saw it was full, then kicked his truck door open and jumped out. He hurried to the scene, moving quickly but not recklessly, his eyes scanning the nearby windows and brush in search of credible threats.

He reached Officer May without incident, but his heart was kicking like a mule, and he was mad enough to murder the world. When he knelt before her, Earl saw a meaty flap of Officer May's cheek blown backward. She was losing blood quickly. He was about to check her pulse when she surprised him and opened her eyes. Her right eye had filled with blood and was swelling closed, but she remained somewhat alert.

"Girls... inside," she muttered.

He voice-texted Gabby, instructing her to get an ambulance to Coach's house ASAP. He told her to say there was an officer down and in critical condition with shots to the face and chest.

Then, looking down at Teresa, he said, "I'll be right back. An ambulance is on the way."

She closed her eyes again; it was unlikely that she'd ever open them again. He stilled his mind, apologized to God for who he was about to become and what he was about to do to everyone responsible for this, and then he kicked in the front door, weapon at the ready.

Afghanistan was hard, hot, and violent; this would not be hot or hard, but it would be violent if something had happened to his girls. The second he stepped inside someone kicked the door shut behind him and cocked a hammer. Earl spun in time to see a teenage boy with a pistol and a scared look.

The kid fired just as Earl ducked; he didn't move quickly enough. The bullet ripped through his right ear, leaving a scorcher of a trail across his cheek in the process.

The shot surprised them both, but the boy was more startled that Earl was still alive. By then, Earl was gone, and Mop Up had taken his place. His answer to the scared kid was a vicious sneer. The kid could have dropped the gun; it would have been good. Instead, he cocked the hammer to take a second shot.

By then, Mop Up was already spinning around, using timing, proper distance, and sound body mechanics to fire off a rage-fueled sidekick. His heel blasted the kid in the snotbox, destroying his nose and snapping his head back so hard that the breaking bones sounded like a gunshot. The kid collapsed in a heap.

Mop Up narrowed his eyes to see what he had done. The kid was a young teen, maybe thirteen or fourteen, so his bones weren't dense and heavy like a man's bones. Had he broken his neck? Definitely. But had he killed him? Yeah, probably. Earl might care, but not Mop Up—he was all about forward movement and momentum.

Farther down the hallway, Mop Up heard bare feet running to the back of the house, followed by a door slamming.

Natalie, Sadie.

The second he scrambled down the wooden stairs and into a gloomy basement, he stopped and looked around, nearly unable to process the scene. The space had been converted to a bedroom, one that looked like the set of some horror movie. And then he saw Coach Tilly and his girls.

The bloodless heathen had a hold of Natalie's head. He put his gun to her head and said, "Come any closer and she's dead, man. You hear me, Earl? She's *dead.*"

"Why are you doing this, Coach?"

Sadie was tied spread-eagle to the bed and stripped to her

underwear. "He's been killing girls like us for years, Dad," she said, her voice hoarse from screaming.

Mop Up carefully moved down the stairs, his .45 trained on Coach Tilly; he talked to the lunatic as he walked down every step to the ground floor, hoping to buy some time while keeping Coach distracted. He only needed to close the distance enough to get a clean shot. In a situation this intense and risky, accuracy was everything.

"That true, Coach?" he asked. "You the guy taking our girls? You the one killing them?"

"This is all just a misunderstanding," he said, a fistful of Natalie's hair in his grip with his gun still aimed at her head.

Natalie was shaking, crying, and looking right at him. Earl wanted to come out and tell her it would be okay, but not until Mop Up did what he was there to do.

Coach jerked Natalie closer, getting a better grip of the old pistol against her head. "I'm not messing around, Earl. You know I can't miss this shot, right?"

"Why *my* girls, Coach? Huh?"

Coach's hard exterior broke, and he suddenly resembled a giddy teenager seeing his first set of breasts. "Look at them, so young and innocent," he purred.

Mop Up moved into firing range and said, "You have one chance to move away 'fore I make your face into a canoe."

That was when Coach's expression darkened, and he fired the weapon. Natalie jumped, Sadie gasped, and Earl froze. But the trigger struck the primer, and there was only an empty click. Coach expected the pistol to fire and Natalie to die, but none of that happened, so he panicked and pulled the trigger again—to the same result.

"You packing your own rounds these days?" Mop Up asked, sliding his pistol into his waistband. "Bad primers happen if you have a run of crap luck, which looks like the case."

Coach turned the weapon on Earl and pulled the trigger twice, three times. Mop Up charged him. Coach dropped the gun, shoved Natalie aside, and tried to maneuver around him. He was heading upstairs to safety, but Mop Up grabbed hold of a sleeve, then an arm, and then he got enough of a grip to yank the older man backward into a blistering elbow strike that caught him flush on the left temple. The old man staggered in a slow half-circle, slack-jawed and moaning, one hand holding his head. He didn't expect that level of pain.

Mop Up blasted him with a ferocious right hook, catching Coach on the chin with an immaculate shot. The old, murderous pervert fell like a sack of rocks.

Mop Up went and hugged Natalie, who was comatose and smelled like urine; he fished a set of keys from Coach's pocket, found the right one, and removed her bindings. He did the same for Sadie, who hugged him so tightly he didn't want to let go. But he had to let her go because this wasn't over.

"Head upstairs and go for help," he said. "If you don't see your mom out front, call 911, tell them who you are, and tell them you have an officer down at Coach's house next to ours."

Sadie nodded and took Natalie with her. The father in him slid backward in his mind once more, allowing the killer to resurface and control the body. Mop Up, back in control, narrowed his eyes and looked at Coach—the big faker, the disgusting pervert. Fortunately, he was still unconscious.

Instead of ending him right there, Mop Up glanced around the room, his eyes landing on a large, rickety-looking dresser. He walked over to it, pulled the top drawer open, and found handfuls of children's clothes, most blood-stained. Then, he opened the bottom drawer to stacks of scattered photographs, a whole drawer full of them.

"Oh, sweet Jesus," he muttered.

These were sick photographs of young girls, most dressed, but some naked and dead. He saw videotapes, too, and shuttered at the sight of them. And then he saw a familiar face looking back at him from a single photo: Mandy Coontz—one of the missing girls.

Behind him, he heard movement and groaning and turned in time to see Coach Tilly coming around. Mop Up stood, pulled the revolver from where it was uncomfortably tucked into his waistband, and thumbed back the hammer.

"You sick, twisted son of a bitch," Mop Up hissed. "How long have you been killing these girls?"

"Long enough," he grumbled, pulling himself to his feet. He smiled for posterity's sake, but Earl had caught and broken him, leaving him ready to surrender if only he could stand without falling over.

Mop Up took a menacing step toward him. "The law won't know what to do with you, but you'll get your fifteen minutes of fame."

"Took long enough," Coach said before letting out a phlegmy cough.

Mop Up cut the distance between them in half, the .45 in his hand at his side. "Guys like you get off on the publicity. For a minute, you matter, but in an infamous, hated sort of way. The courts will try to give you justice, and I know I should let them, but you took my girls from me and Gabby. You were going to hurt them, film them, and kill them for all I know."

"Maybe," he grinned, answering in a vile, syrupy voice. The overhead bulb cast long shadows down Coach's face, making the man look like the monster he had become.

"How could you walk alongside us all night, searching for the girls, knowing you had them stashed at your house the whole time?"

Coach laughed, rubbed his chin and jaw, and said, "How many times you think I did this, Earl? A few, I can tell you."

"You shot Officer May."

"Twice."

Coach finally raised his hands, placed them on his head, and said, "Call Skip if you must. I won't resist."

"My phone's dead," Mop Up lied. "How many have you killed? For real?"

Coach's face broke into a slow, sadistic grin that touched his electric-blue eyes. It was the kind of joyful look a guy like him had when reminiscing every kill.

"Twenty or thirty, I guess? God, Earl, there were so many. Hell, it might even be a dozen more than that." Then he laughed and said, "Man, Bundy or Dahmer ain't got *nothin'* on me."

Mop Up couldn't take it any longer, so he raised his weapon and fired a round into the man's face. The .45's report was as loud in that small space as the damage was bloody. Coach collapsed, dead, but Mop Up stood over him and ran the wheel, putting five more bullets into that bastard's face.

No one should see his face or have to listen to a single word he had to say, let alone make a miniseries and half a dozen movies about him and his crappy, fraudulent life. Guys like Coach Tilly needed swift, brutal justice; they didn't deserve glorification from the press, a place in the history books, or a bio to be studied or envied by losers and lunatics for decades to come.

When he looked up, he saw Natalie standing at the foot of the stairs, her face filled with horror. "It's okay, sweetheart," he said, walking to her. But when he reached for her hand, she pulled it away, backed up, then turned and hurried up the stairs.

Later that day, after they loaded Officer May into an ambulance and off to the hospital, the chief and his L.T. showed up at his house to arrest him.

"I did this town a favor," Earl argued.

"Told you not to bring out Mop Up," Skip replied. "Town's already talking about how you killed Coach. No one knows you killed his kid, too, but now we have to tell them something. You know the kind of shitstorm you started?"

"You saw the pictures in the dresser drawer," Earl hissed. "You and your department have to answer for those girls, Skip. Their deaths are on you. Coach Tilly and his stupid kid are dead because you didn't do your jobs better!"

His former Army buddy ignored him and said, "The courts will decide that, Earl."

"You realize this is wrong, don't you?" he asked as he was turned around and put into handcuffs.

Gabby and the girls rushed to the door, Gabby cussing up a storm and the girls crying all over again.

Skip and his L.T. ignored them; he was still lecturing Earl. "All those girls in the bottom drawer of that dresser, their families will never see justice by trial because you were greedy with *your* version of justice, you selfish old goat. You should've let us do our jobs."

"That murderer deserved what he got, Skip, and you know it!" Gabby shouted. "Besides, he was planning to kill my girls before you even knew Teresa got herself shot."

"Everyone deserves justice, Gabriella, and that's only possible if we uphold the rule of law," Skip said without emotion. "Your husband did what he did for *his* gratification, and it robbed other parents of seeing justice served. The man was a son of a bitch for sure, but he could have led us to his other murders, helped us close more cases, and he ultimately could have answered the question so many families are still asking: where is my daughter?"

"Fine," Earl said, shaking his head in disgust despite Skip being right. "Do what you need to, *friend*."

thirteen
sadie gray

TWELVE YEARS LATER. *NorCal State Prison.*

My dad got twenty-five years for killing Coach Edmond Tilly and his kid, Eugene. He'll probably get out early for good behavior, but he's not well-behaved, so maybe my optimism has no place here. Either way, time will tell that tale. Had Natalie not testified against him, it might have been less time. The DA and her team, though, were a pack of bulldogs, relentless in their pursuit to make Earl pay. So, when they put Natalie on the stand, it was all over for Earl. They backed my sister into a corner and made her say Coach Tilly had his hands up when our dad killed him. With his time at the Agency and his exemplary service record, that was all she wrote.

The judge said, "You knew restraint in your wartime activities but failed to display it here, Mr. Gray. I have no other choice but to make an example of you. There is no place for vigilante justice in a world governed by clear and specific laws, and so now, Sir, you must pay the price."

Less than a year later, my mother drank herself right out of custody. Natalie and I became wards of the state, got split up by child protective services, and haven't seen each other since. There's not much I want to say about my foster families because those were different times in my life—more nightmares. But there is one thing I'll say: there is no substitute for my birth family, problems or not.

I haven't seen my real family since my mother lost custody of us. That ends today. I'm ready to see my dad again. It will be the first time in over a decade. He's written to me a dozen times, but I didn't read his letters until after I graduated from the FBI academy in Quantico. Last night, before coming here, I read each one and cried until dawn.

How did my life take such a drastic turn? That was the question that shaped my life. A therapist would call it my defining tragedy; Earl would say it was life kicking me in the nuts. My mom would pontificate and get drunk. Natalie would tell me to quit being a baby and live my life.

So, on an unseasonably warm Wednesday morning, I enter NorCal State Prison, a supermax facility in Vacaville, California. I follow all of their rules and protocols to the letter, then wait in a large visitor's room with two prison guards. When I see Earl, the second I look at him, my entire face breaks into a smile. And then we both start crying.

He sits at a plastic, cream-colored table across from me and takes my hands. Then, he wipes his eyes and says, "My God, Sadie, you look fantastic. I see you in there, the little girl, but she's hidden pretty well by the woman. How old are you now?"

"Twenty-six."

"You come alone?" he asks. I nod. "Natalie?"

"Mom lost custody of us after you went in. I haven't seen her since then."

"She alive?"

"Don't know, but I'll have the resources to look soon enough."

"What do you mean?"

I swallow hard, having dreamed of this moment for years, and proudly say, "I just graduated from the FBI academy, Dad."

His eyes shoot open. "Holy cow, you're a Fed now?"

I nod again, grinning. "I'm waiting for my field office assignment."

"Did you put in a request?" I indicate that I have with a subtle nod. "Where?"

Deep breath, I tell myself. "Back East."

He snorts and drops my hands. An uncomfortable silence grows between us, and I see more things are on his mind, not just where I will land. Finally, he looks up and asks, "Do you think what I did was wrong? I'm sure you had plenty of time to think about it."

I've thought about that situation plenty over the years. I spoke about it in psych evaluations and to a special agent in charge, who didn't tell me which field office he was calling from but said it was necessary.

"Yes," I answer. "I think what you did was wrong." For what he did to save me and Natalie, I feel like an ungrateful child who does not get it. But I do. Still, as I watch his face sink and sadness pass through his eyes, I'm not done speaking. "Of course, that's what I told everyone, and I'll tell everyone who asks the same thing."

"But?" he asks, eyes rapt.

I take back his hands, aware that the guard has moved closer to ensure nothing illegal passes between us. "I wanted that monster dead, Dad," I lean in and whisper. "I'm glad you did what you did. I'm only sad that Natalie got to watch you kill him instead of me."

A relaxed grin breaks over his face, but emotion quickly overcomes him again. "I did that for you," he said with a snag in his voice.

My dad's statement rocks me; I pull back and let go of his hands. "You... you did it for me?"

He nods despite my reaction and meets my turbulent gaze with insistent eyes. "I did it so you and your sister would never have to worry about him being alive, out there, still... *thinking* of you two, or me and your mom."

Relief washes over me, and I realize how badly I've overreacted. My dad did what any good father would do to protect his family: he killed the boogeyman.

"How do you like it here?" I ask.

"It sucks ass."

"Yeah," I chuckle. "I saw this place on the news."

"Really?"

"The killer ex-cop," I say, recalling a recent story. Earl nodded like he knew the one. "I guess some lunatic ex-cop went off the rails and gunned down three kids in front of a middle school."

"Ah, yeah... that would be Atlas Hargrove."

"You see him in here?"

"Saw him once," he said. "He beat some asshole nearly to death in the chow hall on his first day. Other than that, the dude spends a lot of time in solitary confinement."

"Well, watch your six, Dad. Guys like that are violent and unpredictable."

Earl smiles at my use of words. Then he says, "I'm going to get out of here one day."

"Just make sure it's not in a body bag."

He chuckled again at my honesty. Natalie always expressed too much candor; maybe I'm like her now.

"Have you spoken to your mother?" he asks, broaching the subject.

Slowly, sadly, I shake my head. I'm still trying to forget about her and what she did. "Do you remember Officer May?" I change the subject to ask.

"How could I forget her?"

"She's still with GVPD but working cold cases now. I spoke with her a while back and asked if she could find Mom."

"What do you mean, 'find Mom'?"

"Natalie and I grew up in foster care because Mom got drunk after your trial and ended up hospitalized with alcohol poisoning.

They pumped her stomach, but she almost died. The state took Natalie and me away. She didn't try to get us back. A few years back, I heard she's still alive, but... I don't know..."

Earl sits back in horror and lets out a weighted sigh. "Good Lord, Sadie. I... I didn't know."

"I figured you had it hard enough without knowing that little detail," I say as sadness takes its turn with me. "We all needed to escape our burdens, even if that meant not acknowledging them."

"What about Skip?" he asks, changing the subject.

"Chief Davenport?" I ask.

He nods.

"Drank himself to death five years ago."

"Serves him right."

"Sorry to give you all this bad news."

He mulls it over and cautiously says, "It's all right. I'm just so happy to see you. And I'm so proud of you for what you've overcome and who you are."

The compliment warms me, but there's more in his expression. "Something else on your mind, Dad?"

He nods, still measuring his words. "If one day you feel that darkness creeping up inside you—"

"I won't," I say quickly.

He leans forward and pins me down with his eyes. "You're my child and your mother's child, which means your DNA is probably corrupt somewhere."

"It's not," I say, defiant.

"If that dark day comes and you think you can get away with serving justice *my* way, think carefully."

"Still trying to decide if what you did was right?" I ask. He sits back and nods once. "Don't worry about me, Dad. I joined the FBI to stop vermin like Coach Tilly before they go off the rails."

"You tell me not to worry, but I worry every day."

The guard steps in to tell us our time is up, something that doesn't surprise Earl. *Wow,* I think to myself, *that was quick.*

"I'll let you know where I land," I say, standing up.

"Please do," he replies, standing with me. "And don't be a stranger."

I glance at the guard and ask to hug my dad. He thinks about it for a second and nods, which is unexpected.

Earl pulls me into a deep embrace, not wanting to let go. I do the same because my dad is a mean man, but he loved me enough to protect me and Natalie and suffer the necessary consequences to do what he thought was right.

I finally let go, wipe my eyes, and say, "I love you, Dad."

He nods and says, "I love you, too, kiddo. More than life itself, even when life was good."

"Life was never that good."

"But I loved you and your sister," he smiled, running the backs of his hands over damp eyes. "I still do. Your mom, too—every day."

I try not to, but I cry on my way out of the prison, thinking my only saving grace in this life is that I'm finally leaving California. I cannot wait to leave the bad memories behind, even though it means leaving my entire family, too, if they're even in the state anymore.

Emotionally exhausted, I climb into my car and check the messages on my phone; I have a message from a man identifying himself as SAC Graham. He said he was the agent who called and asked me what I thought about my father's case.

"The bureau has assigned you to my office, the Sacramento field office," his message says. "It's located in the nearby city of Roseville, which you will see when you look up the address. You'll start in a week. Welcome aboard, Special Agent Gray."

The news is a gut punch, but the effect lasts briefly. It would seem as if I'm not yet finished in California. Looking up and around, I try warding off the anxiety of not getting my way, but the moment it hits my chest, the betrayal sucks the air from my lungs and leaves me feeling sick. I hit the steering wheel once with my palm and then repeatedly until the outburst leaves my hand aching in some places and numb in others.

When I finish acting like a petulant child, I break into tears in my car right there, in the prison parking lot. It takes a few minutes for me to pull myself together, and when I do, I glance up and see a pretty blonde woman walking past me. She looks like a supermodel, poised and radiant, put together like a queen. I want to look like her as an agent, even though she's white-skinned, blonde, and likely not a Fed. Still, her look is hypnotic and a bit intoxicating.

The woman turns and catches me staring at her, and then she looks away without breaking stride, severing our brief connection. I turn to the SUV from where she came and see a good-looking man who resembles the blockchain millionaire Leopold Wentworth in nearly every way. He is watching the blonde from an open window. When he sees me, he nods and rolls up the tinted window.

Swallowing hard, I pull my eyes from him and hear myself say, "Well, California, you bright, sunny bitch of a state, Daddy hates a coward." Then I think of how my new SAC said the words "Special Agent Gray," and I can't help the smile on my face.

Feeling hopeful for the first time in a long while, I start my car and say to myself, "It'll be okay. We're going to be okay, Sadie-girl."

THE END

Join Special Agent Sadie Gray in her debut novel, the gripping FBI mystery titled, *The 34 in the Floor*, or head back to Amazon and check out the full listing of books in this series, as well as those books on pre-order. If this is your first look at Sadie Gray, turn the page for a sneak peek at *The 34 in the Floor*, her first case and a book early readers are calling "breathtaking" and "one of the best books of this writer's career!"

the 34 in the floor: a look ahead...

When the past and present collide, murder becomes as easy as breathing...

Deep in the majestic Northern California woods, hidden in a remote hunting cabin, lies a secret too shocking for words: a mystery that could shatter FBI Special Agent Sadie Gray's entire world.

Grass Valley, California, is home to all sorts of people, their darkest secrets, and the shadows where they hide them. It was also the location of a series of abductions, including Sadie's abduction, spanning back nearly twenty years. But when a terrifying discovery sparks a murder investigation unlike anything this quiet community has ever seen, Sadie will be dragged back into the nightmare she fought her entire adult life to escape.

The national media and true crime enthusiasts dubbed the case "The 34 in the Floor", but the FBI hasn't faced a serial killer this prolific in decades. For Sadie, this chilling investigation marks her first case and a return to a home she vowed never to revisit. While no one should have to crawl this deep into a murderer's head to stop him from killing, Sadie will be pushed to the brink, but there's no quit in her, and no lengths she won't go to solve the case and catch the killer.

Grab your copy now at Amazon.com!

also by r.b. schow

THE SADIE GRAY SERIES (*w/ Bailey James*):

THE 34 IN THE FLOOR
THE SIGHT UNSEEN (*December 10, 2024*)
THE BROKEN GIRL (*January 5, 2025*)

THE COMPLETE ATLAS HARGROVE SERIES:

THE TEARS OF ODESSA
THE BEASTS OF JUAREZ
THE BETRAYAL OF PRAGUE
THE DEVIL IN COLOGNE
THE BUTCHER OF CARACAS
THE MARTYR OF NOGALES
THE CAPE TOWN MASSACRE

about the authors

Million-copy selling USA Today best-selling author R.B. Schow is the mastermind behind the pulse-pounding *Atlas Hargrove* thriller series. A second-degree black belt and adrenaline junkie, Ryan thrives on crafting fierce, flawed characters who battle impossible odds. His stories are rich in character development but also packed with plenty of chaos, where the lines between right and wrong blur, delivering gripping, high-octane adventures at every turn. He and his wife live in California.

Bailey James, her husband, and their two little ones live in the Sierra Nevada foothills in Northern California. Surrounded by many small towns rich in history and intrigue, Bailey immerses herself in true crime culture, drawing inspiration from more than a few local, unsolved mysteries. Her writing journey began in editing and has evolved into crafting fiction, with a focus on capable yet realistic heroes and heroines, formidable villains, and the unique charm of small-town life.

Leveraging decades of fascination with true crime, Bailey joins forces with bestselling author R.B. Schow to create high-stakes stories that captivate even the most discerning mystery enthusiasts.

About The Authors

For more information about the authors or to chat with them about the current books, upcoming releases, or cover reveals, be sure to join the private Facebook page, called *The Edge of Your Seat Book Nook!*

Made in the USA
Monee, IL
13 February 2026

44109415R00056